T0159092

THE FICTIONAL ODE

THE FICTIONAL ODE

O.J. SIMPSON SAGA RECAPPED

CLARENCE G. HANLEY

authorHOUSE®

AuthorHouse™
1663 Liberty Drive
Bloomington, IN 47403
www.authorhouse.com
Phone: 1-800-839-8640

Published by AuthorHouse   09/05/2012

ISBN: 978-1-4772-6596-3 (sc)
ISBN: 978-1-4772-6595-6 (e)

Library of Congress Control Number: 2012916120

Any people depicted in stock imagery provided by Thinkstock are models,
and such images are being used for illustrative purposes only.
Certain stock imagery © Thinkstock.

This book is printed on acid-free paper.

CONTENTS

SYNOPSIS

It's satire and should not be considered otherwise —unless in part and in many ways, humoristic. It is also a microcosm of American humanistic ways and habits. I acknowledge that there are in no ways, or doubts, that I as a writer of satire will want nothing else, but for you the reader to chuckle here and there in these writings. Overall . . . this book is contrived as fictional, but is taken from real life events as the author ciphers conditions from the world around him and from the media.

Most of this book will be about the Simpson trial, Christian hypocrisy, American pessimism & polarization, our politics . . . and what we love and portray. All will be a microcosm of 'We the People' from a minority perspective.

What will be very deniable however . . . but the truth will be known . . . we love money in this country and the life it provides for us—giving Satan hands up on winning the Christian war versus the love of money. Don't let anyone tell you differently, or they will be lying to you—and we are very good at lying when this subject of Christianity is imposed and compared to love versus money and influence.

This book will be a different read from others, but it is worth the time and effort even as it is coming from a minority Middle Class American perspective.

The Simpson trial was considered the 'Trial of the Century' and of the man himself. Orenthal J. Simpson's saga provided a minority American format & snapshot for the true faces of Americanisms. It is sad to say this . . . but many other humanity seeking countries of English speaking dominance—as well as French, German and Latin . . . is fairing far better than ours with humane attitudes for brown and black skinned people. We were supposed to be leading in this area. Don't get me wrong, our country remains progressive minded, but something is seriously wrong with the gut of Americanism when it comes to black and brown people from unlikely corners of our society.

Personal zeal for related contents came to mind when I would proof read this manuscript. Fervor and anxiousness seemed to cringe in my thoughts at times as I read, wrote, and realized that this America may not be all that the founding fathers imagined. Honesty & wisdom appeared to be a far, far cry from the Plato's and the Aristotle's writings . . . where common sense was humanistic, wise, and progressive—or even the pristine words of the Bible where we so notably akin ourselves to with announcements in our constitution and on our financial certificates. I think many of us can be considered hypocrites to wise honest ways in today's activism of law and relationships, and we don't like being called that word hypocrite—even when we may know that we borderline a match to its insignia.

In my stories, there will be some Bible quotes, poems, politics, courtroom drama and courtroom combat. It's the American way and is very notable in our politics of norms. Many words and phrases will be colloquial, perhaps chatty sometimes . . . to which we may say that we have little appetite for; but the truth of it all, psychologically . . . we love it. Just as the Romans loved slaughter in their arenas, we love rhetoric, guns, devastating newsreels, political sports and all of its entertainment. Sounds sadistic, doesn't it? Well you be the judge.

We use the phrase game hunting, but the facts are in, we love killing. We love to read about it. We love to see it in the movies. We love to think killing to be a terrible act of insanity . . . so that we can feel outraged, yet sane ourselves at the same time. It is one way for us to scientifically consider us a separation from our bipolar ways and actions . . . without medication.

For the most part, after a degree of remorse and condolence when a tragedy happens, we take death in stride as if it was just another day in the horizon, and usually very little wisdom is derived from losing love ones . . . and our trends remain the same with very little notice. We are more likely to cry over our dogs and our cats for human satisfaction and grief.

Going on with the trial, you will notice that each play by play will have its own wit, solemn humor, and understanding of our nature and its people . . . as you will soon see. The story never intends to demean the families in the true story, nor in this book—but only the events of the trial and Americanism.

The Trial of two teams
The Head Hunters
The Dream Team

Each team is at battle for their client . . . as hypocrisy drenches the entire American society and across the Seas. Every single person had a motive for their team to win. Each was steeped in hypocrisy. We will tell you more about that inside our stories and variant satire.

The courtroom satire quickly fashions itself into a sporting depiction of ill-gotten jurist prudence . . . as our criminal justice system is viewed through the eyes of the author. It was a game of winners, losers and showmanship. It was our way of life, our system, the O.J. Simpson trial; it was an honest depiction of us.

As the stories unfolded, the satire becomes dramatic and is paced with metaphors, poems, stories, and clichés . . . before waking up to supposed American wisdom, values and expectations going forward. The stories soon envelopes into its own saga as it twist its way through the satire of the trial, more trials, and more devices, social studies, and the awareness's of hypocrisies. Be warned, this is satire. Let's get started.

JOHNNIE COCHRAN; MAY HE REST IN PEACE

Woe is unto the shepherds that destroy and scatter the sheep of my pasture said the Lord. Therefore thus said the Lord God of Israel against the pastors that feed my people: You have scattered my flock, and driven them away, and have not visited them; behold, I will visit upon you the evil of your doings, said the Lord; And I will gather the remnant of my flock out of all countries whither I have driven them; and will bring them again to their folds and they shall be fruitful and increase; And I will set up shepherds over them, which shall feed them; and they shall fear no more, nor be dismayed; neither shall they be lacking, said the Lord.

Behold, the days come, said the Lord, that I will raise unto David a righteous Branch. And a king shall reign and prosper, and shall execute judgment and justice in the earth.

Jeremiah 23:1-6

THE FICTIONAL ODE

* * *

MANY WERE CAUGHT UP IN THE SIMPSON
MEDIA FRENZY
SOAP OPERA BUFFS WERE ASKING WHAT
THEY SHOULD DO
WERE THEY TO RELINQUISH THINKING SOME
OF THEIR THOUGHTS
OR WOO THEIR FOOLISHNESS AND PURSUE

SO MANY PRANCED THROUGH
BALLADS–THOUGHTS OF SATIRE
PRAYING THAT THEIR MINDS WOULD
REMAIN FAIR
THEY DECIPHERED THEIR THOUGHTS
DO'S AND DARES THEY FOUGHT
TRYING HARD TO SEPARATE LOVE HATE
AND DESPAIR

DESIRES OF MANY AND HOPES OF SOME
CAUSED THEMES TO CONVEY HONESTY AND
BIAS THOUGHTS
HISTORY WOULD HAVE IT AND TIME WOULD
TELL
VISIONARIES DENIED ACTUALITIES WITH
NAUGHTS

BLAIMERS HAD BEEN ALL OVER THE PLACE
MAINLY TO HIDE THEIR DEVIANT FAULTS
BUT AS WISDOM WOULD HAVE IT AND AS
TIME WOULD TELL
MOST HAD COME FROM FALACIES OF
HISTORY THAT HAD BEEN TAUGHT

* * *

LIKE COFFEE, I WAS PERKING

Like coffee, I was perking when I woke up this particular spring morning—perking in my head, dreams, and in my thoughts. I had something that I wanted to say that I had not said in my first book, 'An Ode to Satire'. I wanted to say more about the Orenthal J. Simpson's saga.

Many had indicated—with good reason—that the O.J. Simpson's trial was a very good sampling of the world that we lived in . . . here in America—thinking that it was a matrix of race and color, money and influence, sports, etc.; but I also knew that every life's matrix' in America, was not a monolithic one . . . and that it was more of a compilation of many American factions and a mixture of Americas human complications—religion, faith, race, and past history.

Those who had indicated that the Simpson Trial was simply a sampling of the world we live in, had some premise of value—but it goes deeper than the surface. That 'case in evidence' had sparked an ongoing nature of our society at large—especially at that time in the late 1990's as it has now; and not to forget that most all are immigrants in this country, from almost every nation in the world—not meant to be an indictment however; but notable America has not gotten much better with race relations since the trial—in both thoughts and minds—as evidence more recently by the new Tea Party; and more specifically the far, far Right of the GOP political Party. It seems like politics has sparked the very soul of the old South. The false meritocracy of it all has become nocuous, and very, very visible in many, many camps, and most noticeable in our political system. Something is wrong.

The wishful thoughts, dreams and expectations that our nation was attuning itself to, was to be a merit one throughout; however that has seemingly becoming null, and some factions across this land really want that common sense attitude voided. Many are relishing in wanted to go back to separating the rights of women, people of color, people who don't (quote) "look like us" they say, others are saying, taking our country back, and all has sparked a separatist few and a war of many at heart, and some hate and malice. This ugly far right type is not only calling names, spitting on congressmen, being wild, wild west with guns and disrespectful, but the spiting on a politicians was beyond the pale, and threatening lives was over the top; and for the most part they were having very little fear in announcing their treacherous thoughts through public announcements, radio's, and public gatherings. A once thought sane country to visionaries who were seeking to become American citizens, and those that the world has looked up too, cannot easily be thought sane anymore. Something is clearly wrong.

Our democracy in which our talents have been paramount in the progression of leading the world in education, science, various arts, industries, is rapidly eroding. We are not making it a priority of moving ahead on the basis of good sense, democracy, achievement, etc. We have gone back to choice ciphering, and of course this can be a hindrance when it is done by ethnicity, gender, etc., but it is also being done by religion and nepotism. We have some serious problems in this country—some serious problems of hatred and lacking of mega love.

This book capsulizes the intricate of Americans true and tried hearts—that all sides have a racist nature and are far from Christian expectations—to which is hard to admit for many. The Simpson Trial had said it all and was a very good sampling of our hearts, minds, and our attitudes.

A Black president has yet sparked that same non-Christian attitude. Something is very, very wrong in America . . . and what is most sad, is that there are so many white and ethnic Americans alike, struggling and giving up their life in some case . . . to right the wrong—no pun intended here, but expected to be noted.

There have been major historical times in our history that matter toward advancements in our behaviors, culture, and our nature. Other times in our history were historical, during their periods of time. Martin Luther King was a major milestone for all of us—even as many have made it their life energy to reverse his theology of life. Abraham Lincoln, Jesus Christ—though Jesus was not birth on this particular land, but the point that I wanted make remains—is that—we kill the good to keep Satan steadfast. We simply operate better this way, and more to our satisfaction. We are not who we claim to be as a Christian nation and something is wrong.

Why do I continue to say that something is wrong? Well it is very simple; the Aurora movie theatre tragedy in Colorado was just another single example. It was a mass shooting and killing of many innocent people—by a very intelligent person which should make us all take notice. Further concerns are that the tragedy was being sorely masked by every single politician who was frightened of the NRA—the National Rifle Association—and their guns. I will not go into the misery of this organization and the tragedy it has cost so many families, but making a note is paramount. However, I am amazed that the politician is supposing to there to protect its people . . . when in too many cases they are our citizen's worse enemies.

Still yet . . . every single politician had continued masking every single word that they were saying about the Aurora incident. Their words were geared toward the rights to bear arms. In other words, to kill something—yet they would say . . . to protect.

Well my words may not mean very much, but I say . . . this right is completely ludicrous—and crazy. I can say unequivocally however, that the guns did the killings; and they will continue to do the killing over and over again; and as long as we pretend that our Constitution and it words will forever hold strict constructionist meanings and cannot be tweaked; it will remain a fact that those words in the Constitution will continue to kill innocent people until that very constitution will soon kill us all—if not tweaked; and further . . . .

If the founding fathers meant for the Constitution to be so very strict, then I am two thirds a human being and have no equal rights in this country at all—to vote, use public facilities, marry out of my race; etc., etc., and etc. You see . . . my skin is black and the Constitution had said I was two thirds a human being, well . . . I think we should speak to God about that issue, but for now, where is the common sense about our actions as human beings. I continue to say that something is very, very wrong in this country.

The Simpson trial versus the beloved people in my country has become even more cynical than had been in their past. For instance, there are many who have a pure hate for the Obama's, not because they are just plain good human beings—and they are—but because they are Black. This faction can hardly believe that more than half of the good people of this country put them in the White House, and they are boiling over with disdain, hate, and non-forgiveness for this elective officer—their presidency. They have also taken an ugly disposition in politics . . . in voting contempt charges against an officer and a gentleman of the land—the attorney general, Eric Holder—who had done everything Representative Issa had ask for in a fluke mishap by the previous administration—for something call Fast and Furious (running guns across the Mexican border). As I had said, it was started under the previous administration and was passed on to the Obama Administration where it was stopped. Attorney General Holder stopped this action, but not soon enough seemed the claim of Representative Issa, who seems to have it out for Holder who had aimed his office at correcting the charges of voter fraud—a non-issue. I will not get into the details of that matter. However, I do want to say that Representative Issa had set out to tarnish this man, and hopefully the president through him. History will be very unkind to the Republicans because of this and Representative Issa will have a black mark against him in our history books—in more ways than one. I have no doubt.

My first book was about the unpredictable and renowned athlete to which I wrote in satire. This one is Satire also, and it recaptures the first version along with the nature of our society. I should also say if you did not read the first one, no need, this one will suffice. That version was about people involved in sports, journalism, lifestyles, race, everyday life, and most of all, our jurist prudence system. Don't worry if you did not read that one, this one will cover those issues as well . . . and hopefully this will be a classic feature of America's nature, but one must be free from personalities and biases. Impossible, I know. Perhaps my writings will appear not to be the same avocation and subordinate pursuit that I wish the reader to be. Perhaps we are who we are.

Might you have thought along the way, that maybe our pure system of judgments on others may not be of such purity at all? I know you will not be surprise to hear my perjury and biases as I write those infamous and restoring words of Dr. Henry Lee—the forensic renowned scientist and professional opinionate in the trial, and in my satire story. He famously said "Something is wrong". When honesty and rightfulness are finally at play, we will have to agree—something is wrong in our society, and it needs an examination and a fixing.

Let me clear the air, I said to my friend, who seemed to be all ears as I told him how I felt about a few things we were going through in our beloved country.

He seemed mesmerized and all ears as I continued on—even though I knew he had his on opinion that may have surely been different from mine. However, he was saying very little. It was like I was giving a speech. Perhaps I was. I was surely into a monolog. My emotions were high.

I said, let me be clear my friend, I am coming from a Black and a minority perspective and experience, so you cannot consider me all knowing of everyone's culture, or even why me and everyone else act on Gods stage as they do. I don't know the entire answer my friend. What I can tell you is that

I am passionate about my feelings and perspectives even as I will not always be politically correct of others and the subject matter. I surely believe that I am, and I am sure that others will also have their honest perspectives of their core beliefs as well.

What I can say with fortified truth is that . . . there are lots and lots of crooks, thieves, and liars in our mist and for the most part they will likely have more resources than anyone else amongst us; resources giving them a platform. Some of these people have been taking from the weakest of us since the beginning of time—well our time here in America—and claiming fair and square, and it to be rightfully their own and they use their resources, ill-gotten clout and their platform to promote their belief and to increase their wealth. For instance, I honestly believe that the now Tea Party, this type of people is largely made up of Ku Klux Klan members, Nazi Parties, Skin Heads, etc., etc., etc., My question is . . . who else can be so angry against their Brown and Black neighbors and brothers in this county as this type has always been. George Bernard Shaw gives us a thought to remember and exemplify, but not necessarily are they the same people.

GEORGE BERNARD SHAW'S PHILOSOPHY

I love George Bernard Shaw's historical statement against imperialism. He was back then, the sharp tongued enemy of hypocrisy of the British, (our colonial fathers) in the early 1900's. They had been pillaging the world of its rich resources for centuries—America was to be no different. He said . . . .

Every Englishman is born with a certain miraculous power that makes him master of the world. When he wants a thing he never tells himself that he wants it. He waits patiently till it comes clearly into his head. No one knows how, but he has the burning conviction that it is his moral and religious duty to conquer those who have the thing he wants. Then those things become irresistible. Like the aristocrat he does what pleases him and grabs what he wants; like the shopkeeper he pursues his purpose with the industry and steadfastness that comes from strong religious conviction and deep sense of moral responsibility. He is never at a loss for an effective moral attitude. As the great champion of freedom and independence, he conquers half the world and calls it colonization. When he wants a new market for his adulterated Manchester goods, he sends a missionary to teach the natives the gospel of peace. The natives kill the missionary's, he (the Englishman) flies to arms in defense of

Christianity; fights for it, conquers for it; and takes the market as a reward from heaven.

Hypocrisy in its most pure and Americanized way. Take what you want, say a prayer and believe that God wanted you to have something that belong to someone else, and believe that the Ten Commandments do not apply to you—but only to others. This is the rationale we believe in. This has become the mantra of many—and more likely than not, Shaw's sharp tongue is the influence we have captured in our society—and may live with.

After all, we are of English influence, but it tears my heart to think that I have to say such words in this book and knowing that one half of America and many, many more are in no ways anything like what has to be said in this book; and I cannot forget them. They are Caucasians who have died for the civil rights of all minorities—as well as right versus wrong. They must have been Gods angels, whom he enlisted to do thy will. I do not mean to victimize them in this book. They were the righteous, the fair and honest thinkers, but so much needs to be said of so many others of the wrong track . . . who mean this country no good, but have the privilege of destroying it under god and our Constitution.

The facts are . . . I belong in this country, I am truly not an immigrant, and most others are. My ancestors were brought here against their will and limited rights as a citizen; we have been thriving and forcing our issues and rightful place ever since our ancestors were dumped off those slave ships. We never gave up. We never gave in. We have been called shiftless, brainless, backwards, the ugliness has no end, but we are still here. We are like Gods people of Egypt-land, and at some point the hold that is being held against us will not last forever. We have always known that we would overcome. The battle seems nowhere in a promising sight for to many narrow hearts and minds, but Martin Luther King Jr. said we would get there . . . and no doubt, I am sure we will; but I am not sure in who's life time. We are making giant strides—athletics, businesses, mixed marriages, a Black president, etc., etc. However, that's enough of that as . . . we are taking that inch and making a mile out of it.

MY STORY BEGAN WHEN

I held up a one hundred dollar bill to show my friend and said, can you even imagine how many poor souls, innocent men and women, boys and girls, have been killed for as much of this in any form or fashion that they (perpetrators) could get it (denominations) in—gold and silver and the likes. This has become our nature, perhaps our god, I said to my friend. Carpetbagger types, crooks and thieves will go to the House of God on Sundays and thank their god for this prized possessions'—just as Shaw had explained in those early years when he was trying to make a point. In fact, this type would rather die than live without his ill-gotten possession. Some have tried to take it (their prize possession) with them, to . . . well wherever they might go to their after-life from this earth.

Egyptian prominence took their wealth with them—well until carpetbaggers start digging it up for their personal use. Enough of that . . . We all have our demons. There are no exceptions.

At that moment, I stood up and walked to my bar, poured a glass of wine, thinking while doing so, and never forgetting what more I wanted to say, and perhaps being rhetorical, perhaps more than I realized. I gave my smiling friend a glass of wine and at that moment, I felt the need to go straight to my computer and begin this litany of writings as my friend simply and patiently complied . . . .

What in the hail was wrong with our founding fathers with this gun business, he ranted?

I was writing by then.

I exclaimed to my friend with action words as I turn to look him straight in the eye, can I once again say how passionate I am about my beliefs in this gun business, and why we have this need to always be killing something? I don't understand it either my friend. Even teenagers know that these weapons are only used to kill something, mostly . . . but to protect as well, I continued. But, this senseless killing takes priority over any protectionist argument made in supposing a peaceful country, in such a negative way that it is hard for me to phantom the real advantage in having so many domestic automatic weapons—and here's why. The Bible says, "Thy shall not kill." This phrased ideology has been flipped and flopped to no end to fit anyone's desire to get what each one personally wants out of their space, society, activity, and even its community.

There was a time that I really thought Americans were the most sensible people that I knew around the world. I had been propagandized to no end as a youngster. We were supposed to kill the Indians. These were terrible people. They were the bad guys. They were taking our land. Let me stop and laugh awhile on that one. However, I would beg Santa to bring me some guns for Christmas (maybe right here I should take the Christ out of Christmas) but in any event, I needed those guns. I needed two of them, like Sunset Carson. I needed a black suit, and if that was not enough, I needed a BB gun. Shoot . . . those caps were not killing anything; but when I got my BB gun . . . behold, birds and pigeons were in real trouble. I was a dead shot as a little lad. Some few windows and pant legs were in trouble also—but we will not talk about that. Smile.

Let's see . . . Perhaps the founding fathers were thinking the British were still coming after them, after they had written the Constitution. Of course they (the Brits) finally became civilize and passed a law that prohibited ownership of guns to citizens. I should say that . . . that was a wise decision after so many years of taking from every European country that had the riches that they wanted and had to have to become proper men and citizens. Not to forget that they continue to pillage the riches from continents like Africa. Poor Africa they will say—well I imagine so. Now that's a laugh once again. There is so much to laugh about that when you realize from the start, which are the real culprits, well the least . . . you have to humor yourself.

Hey lets laugh at this one . . . when most will say that they are Christians. I say no to early settlers, discoverers, and carpetbaggers. But I must agree and say . . . they should have not allowed lesser citizens to read and learn if they were going to keep this stuff a secret . . . and if no one but the aristocrats could read, write, reason and rationalize this stuff, then others would never know the history of it all, and the real culprits. Then they could belie sanctification to the rest of us.

When I am reading the scripture, I recollect that many will say that all is up for interpretation, but still I capsulate this great book as to whom we really are as a human race. When anyone is leaving it up to interpretation, it become easy for me to decide which hypocrite is blowing smoke, because interpretation is a choice. The trouble is that everyone is blowing smoke . . . so much smoke from everywhere that the cloud of smoke simply has clouded out any good sense and logic to good scripture. Everyone has interpretations.

Hypocrisy from everywhere has taken over. The pulpit is not excluded and very seldom exalted. Some of these human people are a disgrace to the God they say that they love so deeply. Shouldn't we laugh some more. After all, I am writing this book in satire. We need a laugh or two to replace the hypocrisy we wade and waddle in each and every day—so don't think me to be clean of such either, but some exposure is necessary for all. After all, remember all those guns I got for Christmas and me not telling you where many of those BB's landed.

Let me say this. I am presently in one of those silly seasons modes—second term seeker, Barrack Obama for president—and I have never seen such a host of lying Christians (can't seem to get that capitalization out of that word when I want it out. I tried to make that word with a little c, but my spell check changed it—another crook I suppose).

In all of my adult life . . . adult life because I never got everything as a little person that Santa promised, nor was he who he made me believe he was . . . I am finding that adulthood has turned out to be a farce of many past beliefs for a little Christian boy who believed this stuff the nuns were teaching him about truth and honesty—and this Santa Claus. It was all fun and game, and I loved every minute of it. Flying slays, chimneys, red nose reindeers, somebody's birthday on the 25th of each year. I am not trying to kill the myth, but I got tired of my spirit being killed after a while when the light became a little bit brighter. (Oh . . . I had better say it now, I loved Sister Ann Elizabeth. She was the best). I just started to grow up a little and express myself.

So . . . the liars never quit however; and politics is the hyper myth of it all; and each of us is expected to live a fruitful honest life in the eyes of our human judge—called grown-ups. Please give me a break, but can we also giggle a bit on this one also? It is odd that proclaiming to be Christians, that in many corners of white people from the older guard . . . they have had little love of patience, respect of awards to the genesis of slaves descendants—perhaps forty acres and mule would have been a start.

Slave descendants have carved their way from scratch . . . to somewhat acceptance, and too many young black men had tried to raise themselves up in the model of the Brits and the founding fathers—carpet begging in their communities. Of course those ways were soon made against the law; and since city fathers were ahead of this 'gaming of the system' as they had done, they simply started building great big brick buildings with barbed wired fences and a plan to house as many black and minority boys as they could—both to reduce their seeding this society, and the inherent use of malice from their founding fathers.

Slave thinking mentalities have blossomed into hate and disdain for natural brown and black skinned people in some resounding corners, especially when they have had hair that is a little less straight and they are just a little too dark.

This supposing Inferior race of people who have done ample more than was humanely required as slaves and many times put upon in inhuman ways that has led to the growth of a nation of agricultural wealth; to one nation of people and a miscegenation to the other; and yet a demise of their human spirit to their descendant. With this growth and wealth for today's white affluent from slavery, the Black race has been decimated to a held back timeline; and a history of the unrewarded, little appreciation and non-acceptance, in a society who has advanced richly, so fast, and so abundantly, in agricultural and at little cost, yet a very heavy burden on a race of people still yet unwelcomed. Something is wrong.

I am speaking of black and brown human beings who know that God loves them, but many times have been treated less than animal—many love dogs and cats. These animals in some cases have more stringent and positive laws in their favor than descendants of slaves in America; and have at times been superior. Stray cats and dogs him quickly move into civil society and with many laws to protect them from harm. I am not sure about minority human protection. You see, I think drugs and those who are sick from such addiction should be cared for. Our society has decided differently—to incarcerate the many, and somehow think they are doing what is right—when we know it is wrong. There has to be a motive for this action, and many of us know what the motive is.

Wealth and money in many cases has forms the core and belief to so many and to such degree that—no less—has to have been consider to be emblematic of their god—to which the power and force of every action taken, is paired to his coffer. Shoot . . . I am sure this type will be taking his coffer with him when he is called to the 'happy hunting ground'. I have no doubt that St. Peter will take a deposition on all of our actions and some will have a lot more pages than others—and without good answers.

Such demonstration of a lack of human rights to the descendant of slavery will remain unabridged in human rights on American history and will continue to be written and spoken about for yet generations to come. Sadly . . . this type lives by a code called a constitution that he follows when it please him, and deactivates his code when it does not meet his pleasure. In fact, it is laughable, that the gods can be his cornerstone and mantra to him, and that he will call himself Christian. Something is wrong. The Simpson stories begin.

RE-ENACTMENT OF THE
SIMPSON SAGE

. . . The girl, she was saying, "I SAW IT, I SAW IT ALL."

"Wow!" I said to myself. "Had she?"

The young lady who walked into my office was a stranger. My assistant had taken the liberty to inform me that she had seen her around the complex before, but that she didn't know her either.

Barbara, my assistant, had not been able to extract or ascertain the full reason for her visit. Seemingly, she was an upper-crust type. She simply wasn't conforming to our strict policy, which was very noticeable at the front entrance. The sign said, 'YOU MUST HAVE AN APPOINTMENT.' It was in big bold letters and she could hardly have missed it. In addition, Barbara had this odd feeling—that maybe I should see her. This was very unusual for Barbara, because she was always protective of office business and office rules. But to Barbara, this young lady seemed to be on a purposeful mission—a mission that had a memorable message written all over the messenger's face. So Barbara thought I should take a closer look. The insight of Barbara, my assistant, had wisdom. She believed that this was a single moment in time when it was okay to bend the rules. She did and she was asking for my approval. At that point of notice, even I was both curious and apprehensive.

I had been a Senior Editor for some few years. Had written a few books, but only one was a best seller. Now I was the Editor-In-Chief and Senior Vice President of one of the largest book publishing company's in the country. We were always looking for a best seller in this genre. In fact, we were looking for the sale of the century. We were in the mass marketing business and Barbara was very much attuned to our mission.

This young lady seemed to be looking to talk to an executive of our company, and had somehow made her way to the right place—several times I should say. I found this out later on. So, when Barbara had finally asked her what her reason was for being there, the lady reciprocated more of an answer to Barbara than Barbara had verbally received. In any event, she knew this lady was on a mission. Barbara's very mode of understanding and her wisdom to envision great publishing possibilities left me no other choice.

"Send her in," I instructed.

"Hello Mr. Haley!" she exuberated as she entered my office.

I noticed that she was a lovely person as I looked up and exclaimed. "Just call me John. We are all very informal around here unless we need to be otherwise." I proceeded to inquire. "Your name is . . . Miss . . . ?"

"Call me Marci," she quickly insisted.

"If you so insist. How may I help you, Marci?" I responded.

I had no idea at this time, that I was about to engage into a most bizarre story, perhaps since the trial that had inspired the Fugitive. I thought??? This is one of those . . . he didn't do it stories, or maybe he did and they're not telling.

"I must share my story with someone before it consumes me," she seemed enforced to say . . . .

Personally, I was vacuous at first. This business sometimes calls for detachment. As a writer, I sensed that the time had come full circle—concerning this particular issue and this story. It was now time for me to get off the satirical merry-go-round I was on. I had been on it for several weeks now—maybe months. It seemed like years.

As Marci begin to share her seemingly single, secret, homicidal story with me, I was anesthetized. Perhaps it was all in her approach, but she got my attention fast. I was already being cannibalized by the frenzy of all this, this so-called, '**Trial of the Century.**' In this so called Trial of the Century, several issues were being conveyed. There had been many chances also, to poke fun at the system

3

and raise numerous other issues that concerned the society at large. Common sense, in this trial, was absent. It had little to no civility—well, that's the way it looked to me. Worldwide audiences had chosen sides, (countries too). They were playing their champions to the tune of, a game-of-sorts. Common sense was not there either; nor had any literary bells been rung—not with our company anyway. As far as we were concerned, we were going to leave this frenzy to the pundits and their followers. But . . . this potential client seemed to have something else to offer. She had said, "I SAW IT," so, I thought I should listen. No one before had ever said, they actually saw the homicide. And that's what had been missing in this trial of circumstantial evidence.

*Some social issues from the most un-common, sense-of-the-word had surely edged a place in our business before. It had come from such odd and single-minded viewpoints and in the areas of **race, spousal abuse, and the justice system**. They all had been promoted by the power of the pen—how cynical, but very true.*

*I thought to myself, how much greater could we all be with every issue that mattered to us, if there were proper usage and intention of the **FIRST AMENDMENT**—the proper usage of the power of the pen, the power of the message.*

From another side of the above issues is, (and the way I had seen everything before I became an editor) when you can control another mind (positive or negative) with single-minded strokes, using the power of the pen, use that power. Use that gift, especially if it was going to bring you financial gain. Financial gain was paramount.

Eventually I learned better, and I no longer wanted the negative powers that journalism could bring, or a writer could provide or imprune. I had always been led by the moral vision of a story, but only from a capitalistic viewpoint. I had been led by capitalism then and nothing else—but that was before. Our company was then, and now, considered honorable in its journalism. But, in many ways and many times, we were tabloid. We couldn't admit that. But let's skip through the chase, our credibility was there, sometimes our pens were not, and that's the bottom line. We were many times, sloppy and we got away with it. I'm sorry to admit this now.

This O.J. thing was perhaps timely for our questionable society and had been an eye opening opportunity for many publishers to exploit—or rather to help evaporate this society's troubled waters. We knew the power of the pen could do either—but what would we do? Most would be exploitative.

At this moment, it seemed best to let Marci monologue, and I sat back and judged the net worth of what she needed to share with us. My lingering question was, why hadn't she gone to the newspapers, or the police, with this story? Why me? Why our company? I was asking myself. Also, she could have authored her own story if she thought it necessary that her story be told. But, of course, I was determined to hear her story through. Perhaps it would have literary value.

As she began to monologue, she exclaimed, "I SAW IT ALL . . . I saw it all!" Naturally, I assumed she had seen the alleged Brown/Goldman homicides. That seemed to be her reference point even with Barbara. She had told Barbara that she lived in Brentwood—I knew that was the scene of the homicide.

She explained, "I was walking 'LINKS' when she and I came upon this horrid scene. I was frightened, chilled and devastated. I froze in my tracks."

She continued, "There was this dark man who hurried past me and my pet Links. He seemed frightened too! He was covered-up pretty well and at the time, I couldn't make out who he was. I'll tell you about that later on. But, Links seemed to be stalking to the sound of a dog wailing—I wasn't sure. I could hear a howling in the not-too-far distance. It all seemed to have happened so very quickly, but now that I've had time to think, well . . . .

Let me back up and start at the beginning. First, I should tell you, my residence in Brentwood isn't far from the Mezzaluna Restaurant. I frequent the Mezz quite often. I know most everyone there—the owner, the employees and especially the waiters. My location could be considered walking distance, but I never do that, not even when I'm exercising. When I dine there, I usually drive and use their valet parking service, as I did that Sunday evening, June 12, 1994. About the driving, well, it usually lends credibility to my lifestyle."

"I was just leaving the Mezz—having had a gracious meal around 6:30 P.M.—it was when Nicole Brown Simpson and her family size party were making their entry. I saw her, but she didn't see me, and consequently we were not close enough for pleasantries. Nicole had a flare, you know. She was very friendly and sort of a flamboyant type. She was always warm and welcoming to those she knew and came in contact with. We were friends. Females like us have a reciprocating friendship, worldwide. We look after our own. And I had been friends to the Simpson's for many years."

"When you are as friendly as she was, you most surely were going to have some unsavory types—to muddy your water. She did, and many knew this. It's obvious also, that many times, there are folks who put themselves upon you, garner your friendship, but are really after more than just that—more than your friendship, that is. And there were many of those types around."

"As I drove from near the valet parking stand, I noticed two things. One was that Juditha—Nicole's mom—had dropped something. It didn't seem important at the time and I wasn't quite sure what it was. My intention was to call Nicole later on,

perhaps the next day, and mention it. A valet person had picked up the item, I had noticed. But, evidently he didn't have the chance to return it to her right then. Later, I found out that what had been dropped, were her prescription glasses."

"The most disturbing thing from that evening, and it continues to haunt me, was what I think I saw. Four men seemed to be stalking Nicole and her family. They had congregated several feet away and were looking and pointing at Nicole's party. They looked very rough, very threatening. At that time, I could hardly believe what I thought I saw, so I was passive. But now, I'm not so sure that I should have been. I've been wrestling with this issue, now . . . I need to tell someone, because some other things happened also."

"As I drove past the four men who were wearing turtlenecks, I noticed that they were about thirty-five to forty years of age. I remember this fearful feeling I had about their demonic demeanors—that all soon passed. I didn't know any of them. But, I was left with this mental picture of their faces and motions. Those guys were on a violent mission. I believe now that the mission was directed at Nicole's family."

"When I left the Mezzaluna, I went for a short ride. It had been such a lovely evening—an evening made for a ride by the sea. My brand new Convertible Sports Benz 500 SL made such a ride even more enjoyable. It was a clear day, with a temperature

that anyone would envy from any of our United States. It was a perfect evening."

"After my short cruise, down toward the City of Angels—Brentwood is elevated you know—I returned, did some chores at home and took Links for a walk."

*"While **Links** was stalking the keen howling of a dog, I was concerned. But, I simply kept my distance from the direction that sound seemed to be coming from. You see, my pet Links is a pit black Jaguar, having been crossed with a family line of Jaguar, Leopard and Lynx. I named him Links—get it? Lynx lineage. **Links** is female and is completely tamed. But of course, I have always had this deep unanswered query, "Are any animals with lineage from the wild ever completely tamed?" This question came back to haunt me again, when this eerie situation with the howling, confronted me. It hadn't happened before with me and I wasn't sure what to do about it. I was playing every move now by ear."*

"Tamed they may be—these cats have great strength and sometimes a mind of their own, especially when fright alarms them. Usually, squealing sounds, or shrilling cries, or even high pitched waves, seemed to bother Links' behavior. So, naturally, I was concerned. At this point, I was playing by Links' rules. That was all I could do. I don't have Links' strength, you know—and that's an understatement."

"When the tall dark man (I wasn't sure if he was a foreigner) sped by Links and me, I thought that was a good thing. Because I just didn't know what to expect with Links, you know. I never felt I should be isolated or anything like that. And of course, neighbors usually walked their pets around at that time and I could usually see someone, nearby. In fact, I had been following several yards behind Ron Goldman—a waiter at the Mezz. I knew him, of course. He seemed like he was in a hurry. He had distanced himself from me as Links and I stopped during her stalking period and all. I suppose we were less than a hundred yards from Nicole's condo on Bundy, and I was sure Ron had seen the same man I saw rushing by."

"Everything started to be very weird when, a minute later another fellow ran to the other side of the street from the same direction. By that time, Links and I both were in a stalking mode and now I didn't know what was going on, or what to expect next. As far as Links was concerned, I was the follower and she was the leader. Her strength made that so. But she was in a staying mode, which was good."

"What's going on, I begin to wonder as this commotion was taking place. Well, we started to walk on further, and Links seemed to approach each step with a consistent caution. If I had known what I was about to see, I would have turned around and went back the other way. I try to mind my own business in most instances. I'm not married *and my two youngsters are with their dad. That's nobody's business, of course, but female divorcees can sometimes be left with households that are very unsafe. I think about that sort of thing."*

"I realized by now that we were silhouetted in the darkness of the night. Because, as we passed the area of 875 South Bundy Drive, at Nicole's Condo, (we were on the other side of the street) I saw two men seemingly in a tug of war with a third man, who must have been Ron Goldman. I didn't know that then; I thought I should be minding my own business. Hassles go on all the time in this city of angels—some good angels here and some bad ones—perhaps some demon forces, also. I heard L.A. had thirteen homicides that same night. But our neighborhood was usually safe for outings like this. This night was more different than any other I knew before in Brentwood. But, guess what? There was another man in view as this commotion came to an end. He was walking toward the Bundy home of Nicole. Two men started to run, just as the others had before, evidently because they saw that last fellow approaching the scene from the rear. They turned and ran out the front way and further down the street, as the other two men had before."

"I hadn't noticed the bodies yet, but as the other man approached the walk area at Nicole's property, I could hear him say faintly—with remorse and some anger "Oh my God!" Having come from the rear, he then rushed to the front gate, evidently not seeing me or anyone else, as he looked around. He then

went back to the homicide scene. Acting confused, he then simply left the area."

"I got out of there and went straight home. I then called the police. I wanted to tell them everything I had seen. I was making my call around 10:25 P.M. The dispatcher had put me through, but after someone answered they put me on hold. And the more I waited and thought about the surrounding issues, the less I wanted to get involved. Drugs were cropping up in my thoughts. It was an issue with most all of us. In fact, that Faye Resnick person kept flashing in my mind. I was having second thoughts about the whole thing and before someone finally answered at the police detective station—I chickened out and hung up."

"I was so confused that I couldn't sit still. So I got back into my car, took another cruise. This time I took a slow drive down Bundy Drive, by Nicole's condo just to investigate. Perhaps I should have tried to call her, or O.J., or someone else. I simply did not know what to do. So I took this drive. And, guess what? As I drove by, I saw this man. I thought everyone had left. But I recognized this man. He was one of the men I saw earlier. It was Mark Fuhrman, the detective. I didn't know him that night, but later I kept seeing him on television. The one who had said he couldn't take it anymore and something about **Chinks and Niggers**. But, he seemed alone."

"He was doing the weirdest thing, and it didn't seem like police work. As I passed inconspicuously, I noticed him out of my rear window, also. He was carrying something away from the scene with him. He was holding something. By that time, I had gotten further up the street a bit and had stopped and turned my lights out. I noticed he had gotten in his car and had started to drive in my direction. After he had gotten past, I followed him from a distance. He was heading toward Rockingham, which made me wonder. I thought about O.J., but I didn't know what was going on. Later, when I was passing by, after picking up a bit of speed, I noticed he stopped for a while at O.J.'s Rockingham Estate. But, hold on, here's what I saw just as I passed—four other men were already waiting. I didn't recognize O.J. among any of them. They all looked suspicious. One man quickly got in the car I had been following and the others soon drove off behind them. By now, I was really puzzled and confused."

"At first, I could not make out who any of these men were. But, guess what? I remembered later, two of them looked like the men I saw at the Mezz. The only difference, there had been five at Rockingham and six of them at the Bundy location. But I remembered something else I hadn't thought of before—they were all wearing turtlenecks. In this weather and four guys wearing turtlenecks and dark ones at that, was very odd. When I later started to put two and two together, it was adding up to the four guys I had seen in turtlenecks earlier. I noticed *another thing. The car I had been following had official license plates. Official license plates! Now, I was really puzzled. I really didn't know what to do. I was still baffled. There have been so many stories floating around, and I sort of feel the one I am telling will just fly in the wind with the rest of them—plus, I am confused. I think I saw what I saw, but something tells me I didn't see what I thought I saw. And if I pursue what I think I saw, I think I am going to be in big trouble in this so-called city of angels. Mr. Haley, that car had official license plates!"*

"I think the majority of our citizens are the angels and many of our officials are the other guys. This place is not always what we think it is."

"There's more. The next day, the police station called me. They asked me if I had been out driving the night before around Ten P.M., and if I had seen anything pertaining to a homicide. I told them No!—Because something just didn't seem to mesh. The caller then said very stern and candid, "Ma'am, this city can be very dangerous for the best of our citizens; the less we know can sometimes be our best defense and protection. Please let us know if you have a recollection." His voice sounded a little threatening—like cold steel at that time. Something was funny and I must tell you, his voice reminded me of the Asian judge—Judge Lance Ito—I later heard him on TV."

"Anyway, I'm still not sure what to do. I've contemplated over and over again. I remembered you from your best-selling book and when you signed my copy at Stanford University. I was working on my Masters then in political science. It was when you talked about your book, entitled, 'THE CRIMINALS ARE IN THE WOODWORK'. I thought that coming to you for directions, might be best for now."

"That's not all. You see, I've been watching this trial and it's crazy. It's the most bizarre display of jurisprudence I've ever seen. It's a circus. I can't be part of that. My integrity is at stake. And every witness that has gone on the witness stand has been degraded to no end—regardless of their credibility. But, I've been thinking about what I can do for Nicole. My God, her death was gruesome."

"Another thing, I am not so proud of our LAPD. Here's why. I've been stopped by the LAPD a few times. But one time they frightened me with their guns drawn, and they acted quite rough and arrogant. There were several and they all had very bad attitudes. Each seemed to support the other, even when they realized they had stopped the wrong person. They thought I was a drug dealer. Before that incident, I always saw them as my protectors. But since that incident and it takes just one with me, well . . . I'm not so sure about our city angels. Some are really devils in disguise. I've been keeping up with their types. The headlines didn't depict their full closets when they made the

news. Some of those protectors of the law in our society were of the worse kind, and the good ones supported the bad ones sometimes, probably out of fear or comradeship. But, many are very good. Some of the good types will find themselves in the same foxhole with the bad ones and react apropos. Some do the foxhole bit, because their only means of protection are the bad guys. There is nowhere else for that type to go. It becomes a fraternity thing with the good guys and they find themselves clinging to the bad. Then it becomes their survival system. Life has a way of putting one in such a position."

"Since my experience with those soiled angel types, I've developed a different attitude. My experience has made all the difference and it's sad."

By this time and after listening to her monologue for a lengthy period, I wasn't sure whether I had received the entire story she wanted to convey to me. So, I simply asked the big question, "Who were the men? And what did they do?" I was even more curious now. I wanted to know the crux of this story. I wanted some answers to the Simpson saga. Common sense told me that there was more than the eye had seen. There was more to this story—this satire. If this was the Simpson story, did it need to be told with sarcasm, with a different style and a different flavor? Did the cold, cold ice between towns, cities, friends, families, households and acquaintances need to be broken? Should it be done with satire? The homicide itself had been somewhat of a polarizing saga and can perhaps be better understood if we turn back the pages.

The saga was very well demonstrated back during . . . .

A SATIRE ENACTMENT OF THE SIMPSON TRIAL

The Trial of two teams
The Head Hunters—They are the Prosecutors of
the land
The Dream Team—The Defense Machine the
protectors

WEEK ONE

<u>You are presently inside the game of satire</u>

(January 24, 1995)

When opening plays had begun on January 24, 1995, it was very clear that the jury would surely bring back a guilty verdict on the Defense Machine. The opinion of the American populace was generally "thumbs down." Supporters otherwise were saying, "come on, lets play ball." They seemed to be simply, vying for a fair game.

The **GREAT EMPIRE OF LANCE ITO** hollered, "P-l-a-y B-a-l-l." Of course, we found out later. That didn't seem to mean very much. There were too many timeouts, too many meetings, too much posturing. However, the games did actually get started when **Prosecutor, Head Hunter CHRISTOPHER DARDEN** came up to the plate to bat. He got on with a bunt.

18

Many were glad he did because he just didn't seem to grip his bat or stand in the batter's box very well.

It wasn't long before the world's favorite female batting champion, **Head Hunter MARCIA CLARK**, came up from the deck, coveted the batting plate and knocked the ball clean out of Ito Fields. She was batting clean up and clean up she did. It was her first round of play as the crowd cheered her successes, leaving little to no chance left for the Dream Team Defense Machine.

By the end of the first ending (inning) and as far as many were concerned, the Head Hunters score board was all hits, they had all the plays, all the homers, and nowhere left for them to go. It can be made clearer by saying that the scores were two runs, three hits, no errors, and no one left on. The Head Hunters were surely winning this ball game by leaps and bounds. The first half was a sad ending (inning) for the Defense. This was because all that seemed left now was Umpire Lance Ito's final sentencing and decree. It seemed like the Jury was in; the game should be over. They had heard it all. Those whose gyroscopes had been set in favor of Prosecution could be heard cheering throughout the entire free world. The Prosecutor's opening statement had clearly notched an edge in their bats—for a win, of course.

(January 25, 1995)

But, hold on!! This was only the first half of the first inning. The competing team, who considered themselves the **PROTECTORS OF THE CONSTITUTION**, was yet to bat. Johnnie Cochran Jr., who carried a heavy-hitting Louisville Slugger, was first to hurl some bogus, but effective pitches at the Head Hunter's dugout. In fact, there were those who expected that he would at least tie the scores in his opening offensive play. And tie the score he did, and then some! He had never won a homicide series. But he would hurl some exciting pitching experiences at the opposing teams' dugout—before settling down to typical plays. We will tell you more about that later on, but first . . . .

(A LOOK IN REVIEW)

It had been well-reported that the world viewed and listened to these pre-game performances by every means possible. Helicopters, blimps, binoculars, videos, radios and P.A.'s (public announcers), all were a part of the show-and-tell in this game. **It started when Orenthal James Simpson, with A.C. Cowling's Bronco vehicle was breaching the freedoms of the Los Angeles public highways**. Orenthal was supposed to be in custody. He and A.C. were parading the highways and being followed by a **cavalcade of guarding vehicles, THE CUSTODY GANG.**

It was Los Angeles, June 17, 1994. This chase was nothing short of a ceremonial procession. It would be named the 'SLOW **SPEED CHASE**' parade to the Orenthal James Simpson World Series. Displays of bystanders, several turns in the highways—all would become a major part of the games played there at Ito Fields. Dice, Black Jack and many hands of Poker would be played before reaching the final field of competition. But what could anyone expect, this was the Orenthal Series. The world had not seen the likes of such pre-game play. Everyone was jockeying for their most lucrative positions, including Actors, Lawyers, Policemen, Commentators, News Media, etc.—even the jurors. After all, this was the big leagues—a place where professionals were either making it, or breaking it. Some had made it big as new recruits. Others were not doing as well. But before the season is over, many will be cut. Some will be broken; others will yet be reduced from their lifestyles of tranquility, and there will be little or no rest for the weary.

By the time the chase reached Ito's Parks and Fields (courtroom), it all became frenzy, synonymous to a game. Many had grown tired of the media madness. But, they too continued on with a robust taste for the flare, which had been much akin to a media appetite. In other words, theirs was a love and hate affair between them and the media [food for naught].

At that time, these games were coming off approximately six months of discovery and were expected to last up to six months more in competition. No one knew for sure, mainly because of an outrageously long pretrial-in-discovery.

The second highest highlight of the unfolding drama was the slow speed chase back to the Simpson Mansion. Orenthal had threatened his own life. He couldn't seem to take it anymore. Many had asked, "Take what?" He first wanted to visit his ex-wife's grave and then was desirous of his mother's maternal love and attention. [She lived up-state California.] WHO REALLY KNEW HIS TRUE MIND? But many thought the romanticism came early-on as they saw the love of Al Cowlings, who risked his own life to save the life of his dear friend, O.J. Simpson.

As some might have known, Orenthal's first wife was Cowlings' first love. It had been indicated that Orenthal, once a Heisman Trophy winner, had stolen his best friend's girl and married her and later devoiced her. Aside from that, Orenthal found himself in the game of his life—a predicament within frenzy, based on a tragedy and his best friend remained by his side.

All of the **Dream Team** was playing as free agents—very well paid ones. They were Defensive Players. The **Head Hunters**, well . . . they were sort of bought and paid for, with the people's money. They were Prosecutors. As stewards, they had settled in to using as much of the people's money as it would take to hang the main player, the sports star, the accused. They would leave NO stones unturned—but we later found that they did not use every stone that they had turned up. It may have hurt them in the end.

The Head Hunters' owners and overseers had recently been in deliberation as well. Their considerations were being held toward some player release. Discussions were on the table and the vote had not been called for yet. This last undertaking, (Orenthal's Trial) was to be their final review. So this game subsequently became sort-of a do-or-die dilemma for some of the Head Hunter players.

In any event, the blemishing play had become scrimmages at times, but their order of play was very healthy. **It was a good chance to view the system's FLAWS, DEFECTS and SHORTCOMINGS.** There were imperfections, (you will hear about those) and many suspected their dearth, but most wanted to follow their faith in proficiency. The system was to now face the limelight of world observers and a record number of spectators. Our democracy, our sense of fair play, our model, and our jurist prudence system was on display.

Discussions and skirmishes between these two teams, (the Prosecutors and the Dream Team) were being conducted in the American way. It was the system—a Democratic System. All of our games are democratic. But before we begin to delve into the Prosecutor's Team, or the Dream Team's play-of-action, play by play—let us first

Clarence G. Hanley

preface game focus and record some background and history.

(WITH ALL THINGS CONSIDERED)

As a reminder, over one hundred and fifty years ago, our country went to war. It was called a civil war and some human rights were a part of the composition of winning that war. One can argue that the war was a cause and effect of industry against agriculture, or human rights against slavery, or the north against the south, or the union against statehood. Who knows what may have been in each politicians mind at that time. Human nature can be so different in the mind of the believer. After all, we are a nation of immigrants and we each brought with us a different ideological thinking from our heritage. Lincoln, had said "one nation conceived in liberty that all men were created equal" but time has told us that it has been very hard for each man to follow that basic rule. We all continue to think in terms of being better than the next person—our neighbor—even if scripture does not agree. We will cheat on SAT TEST, or any other factor, to prove on file, that we were better than our neighbor.

Let's consider each decade in the nineteen hundreds after Lincolns emancipation, after a promised future and an initial start for African Americans coming out of slavery. Each decade brought on a new and ugly way for one man to show he was better than the other, and is best described with color versus white.

O.J. AND NICOLE

AND SPOTLIGHTING OUR COUNTRY'S HYPOCRISIES

More than seventeen years earlier, two people met and fell in love. They married some several years after their initial infatuation. Orenthal was a Black, thirty two year old icon. Nicole was a White, Seventeen year old princess in her own right. Both would be betrothed to their hearts and dreams.

Some would later ask, "Was this a Cinderella affair or a Romeo and Juliet story?"

"Hardly," others would say.

I will leave that thought to anyone's imagination. By the end of their love and marriage this charade had taken on characteristics of a Cleopatra/Julius Caesar/Mark Anthony spectacle. But for many, this was much more attuned to a Sampson and Delilah saga.

Unlike the spirit of the Roman Empire, America is many times more carefree; so we will liken our story to such. In no way do we intentionally demean the human side of our story. There had been a double homicide before these games started. The ex-husband athlete was on trial **pleading a ONE HUNDRED PERCENT NOT GUILTY plea.** We simply carefree the style in which we tell our story in satire. We aim it at the **SYSTEM OF AMERICAN JURIST PRUDENCE**, which is good, but not perfect.

You see . . . this case really had become a game of sorts. The sadness overall, was that this double homicide, which had been played out in our media system had become a depiction of many facets of American lifestyles. Sad to say, but that was not so good. The entire world had the American justice system on camera and in camera. Each got a clear view of the system's mentality, its people and its society. It would boggle their fantasies of the American Dream and its hypocrisy.

Some nagging faults had been focused on the camera's eye—centered at the heart and core of its people. That wasn't so good either and may have shed more light than necessary on the country's defects and imperfections', which should have been long-gone-away. It should have never gotten that far, especially not in the form and fashion that it did. Not like that in the media, the cameras eye depicting the demise of these two wonderful human beings—Nicole Brown Simpson and Ronald Goldman. This had become an American Capitalist Mess. This was now a media recitation of domestic love and war, money and dreams, color and distinction. With all this on the agenda, Orenthal was being tried for the double homicide—a court that would display and catapult the core of our society to the face of the outside world and its opinion of America and the American Dream.

So make no mistake about it, what was now on trial in this ball game of life was SPOUSAL ABUSE, THE SYSTEM, and PREJUDICE. Because, with a disturbingly high number of American females in shelters or counseling programs for spousal battery and spousal unrest, pro-claimer's were coming out of the woodworks. And there were those who proclaimed to be keepers of the Constitution who were speaking up against the system. Also, there was talk that not all Afro-Americans were victims of bias, but that all Afro-Americans were victims. All of this had caused human rights cantors to be on their watch. The media was now engaged.

UNCONSCIOUS BIAS

It is very easy to forget our unconscious biases. Each of us has this bias, and few are willing to admit it. I bring this up because this tragedy has every element of our society and our unconscious bias. Many of us may be bigots, I don't know.

I remember the day that O.J. Simpson was being acquitted of this homicide. I happened to . . . at the exact time, was showing my aunts home to a real estate appraiser. She was a white female. I was doing a walk thru with her as the announcement was being made on Television.

Not guilty on all accounts. I could see her heart fall. I felt a global relief, and I could tell that she was floored with distraught. I said nothing. Her question had to have been, "how could this be", and my bias was . . . finally, some equalization in our unfair decrees. I did not care whether Simpson was quilt of this crime or not, but I wanted to see a minority win one—just once—in this political climate. I wanted to see this descendant of slave fore-fathers on equal footing with unfair law decent, in a country that can sometimes get it right, but too often get it wrong in their decree against black minorities. My predicate for this particular bias is that there are just too many Black boys and men incarcerated with unfair time; cocaine for White youngsters gets a few months to none; and nearly a life time for Black boys who had crack cocaine in their possession. If they had it on them, there is almost an automatic three count—purchase, selling, and using, and perhaps they were, but what I am bothered by, is . . . why pat one youngster on the back as if he was an accepted entrepreneur, and lock the other up for nearly his entire life because he was not. This had been too often with bootleggers and owners of speakeasies back in the early 1900's. If they had the gavel, they controlled the laws . . . and that is why there will have to be recompense at the appointed time.

(BACK TO DAY TWO)

The Trial

And now back to the games. By now, free agent Johnnie Cochran had taken looks at a few balls, taken a few strikes, fouled some too many times before hitting a long, long, but long home run, for some very big scores. Referee Ito would call some of his runs back, thus reducing his team's scores, before they would take the field again. There was a long timeout to review some of his plays.

These games were being canceled for two days for more discoveries—which should have been concluded. Many season ticket holders were getting puzzled. The jurors knew nothing either. No one seemed to know whether this was some sort of strategy, or tactic.

Was Cochran jockeying for field position for his defense team, or what? Here is what happened. Dream Team pitcher of the year for the Defense, Johnnie Cochran Jr., had cocked several balls for several big throws. He was hurling at the prosecutor's game plan, of course. He did a good job, because by the time he had leveled his bullet curve balls (with some screw-ball English), news was heard and cheered by millions across the Afro plains.

Here are just a few of the curve balls he used. "They cannot close me down, Ref. I'm going to throw my best balls until we present all of our players. The Head Hunters have hurled a campaign of character assassination against one of my teammates. And yes, we do want the good balls on the field and we have most all of them. We want the truth balls to come out and they will in our cross exams and in our defense. The Prosecutors have overlooked some of the good balls—evidence—we would like to play with. My client, my teammate is a victim. He's a victim of bad pitches by the LAPD. When we bat again Ref, we are not going to swing at any more bad throws."

Cochran had also suggested that blood found beneath the fingernails and on the back of Nicole, did not match that of either victim, or Orenthal Simpson. He was suggesting that someone else could have thrown the killer pitch.

By that time, Cochran's client had been summoned to stand before the jurors, his peers and the world of TV at large, to display his scars from previous games of play. The world was perplexed. Not from seeing his scarred knees and his arthritic fingers, but from everything else they had witnessed and heard. However, the Defense explained, "With these scars, Orenthal was too infirm to have thrown the "killer pitch." And that was why his client, the retired teammate, had pleaded not guilty. "The evidence," he indicated, "will show that Orenthal is an innocent man, wrongfully accused of these dirty plays."

Orenthal's exercise videos tapes, well . . . that's another story. **By this time, the world had heard quotes from Martin Luther King Jr., Abraham Lincoln, and Cicero. Cochran, with the Dream Team, was saying, this game had been RUSHED TO JUDGEMENT, with an obsession to win at any cost and by any means necessary.** Many heads dropped. Not only did many heads drop, but one player on the opposing team actually cried real tears before dropping out. The Dream team was later cited for unauthorized alterations in their game plans.

The destroyed Head Hunter, William Hodgeman, and after some arguments about unfair tactics, had **been** later spotted teary eyed outside of Ito's playing fields. The stress was too much for him to bear. He was later hospitalized—rushed to the hospital in the middle of that same night.

Head Hunter Darden was also found whining to the referee and asking to be excused **from** his duty as civil **servant** steward. He just wanted to run away and hide. Referee Lance Ito commanded him to remain in his position, recoup, and finish the game and to act like a leader of his team. After demonstrations of pouting by Head Hunter Darden—things like sitting on the edge of his seat and his displays and interpretations of elementary school **boy** body language—spectators begin to wonder about their public paid stewards.

Only Marcia Clark had remained stalwart, directive, and focused. She was immovable, while the men were falling apart. She was a lady with aim. Her bat, her gyroscope, her pointer, all was aimed at Orenthal. She wanted to see him hanging from the Ito Parks and Fields Scoreboard. And, who would know, her inclinations might have aspired to her wishes—only time would tell. But meanwhile, shy perks of smiles quietly lingered over the Dream Team's Defense Machine and their Camp.

(January 26, 1995)

This day, more discovery discussions about highly technical DNA evidence were a part of the games. This play strategy of evidence is to be tantamount to these games for prosecution. Contamination will earmark the Dream Team's strategy. Garbage in, garbage out—the defense is suggesting. The Head Hunters will introduce the DNA. It is noted that when DNA is tested in medical laboratories, the testing is strictly conducted—and thus the quality is high. A Dr. Mullis will attest to this defense strategy. It seems that when otherwise handled, there can be contamination—anything from sky-high levels to minutely resulting flaws.

The DNA connotation is short for Deoxyribonucleic Acid. It is a complex, two-stranded molecule, wound into a double helix that makes up the chromosomes in every cell of any plant or animal.

Discussions on DNA will be confusing to most lay persons. We will be simple minded and so will our satire. Though it is the theme of the Defense, we will also be sticking to CONTAMINATION, COMPROMISE, and CORRUPTION. This theme will not deduce prosecution's ideology. Instead, it will help us keep the DNA argument simple, interesting and in a satiric mode, aimed toward the system.

(Just to clear the air. *An Ode to Satire* may satirically send some few messages, but sincerely takes no sides.)

(January 27, 1995)

Today, it appeared like the worlds greatest female prosecutor was beginning to look like a cry baby. As Umpire Lance Ito helped Head Hunter Clark through what she called inequities in the games, she was showing signs of feminine inferiority complexes. Had this Head Hunter succumbed to an overwhelming defense? Never, but this new conference was something about her game (plans) being completely used out of context. It seemed to make her a bit nervous and very unsettled. She felt very strongly that her balls (proposed evidence) had been taken away from her and were being misused and misrepresented. I think she was referring to the Dream Team taking every chance in their opening statement to dart little holes in her game—her opening statement.

33

Defenses strategies seemed to be working. At this time in the games, Head Hunter Clark had been asking Referee Ito to have all the balls returned to the referee, so that he could once again issue them equally again. She was also asking to once again be able to display her initial talents that had won the hearts and minds of half the world. Just one more time, she pleaded, just ten minutes will do. I need an even playing field once again. And, once again she got what she asked for. (The author notes that chivalry does have its place.)

Clark had wanted to fashion the field of play to her advantage. She wanted to demonstrate a prosecutor's version to a world wide viewer ship. She wanted a head start.

Clark thought the defense had been unfair and she told the umpire just how she felt about that. She said, "I want them to leave my balls alone. Play with your own balls," she said. The defense's response was, "But this is the way the game is played Miss Clark. Haven't you read the rules?" Of course, Ms. Clark knew the rules, but somehow at this point and time, things just didn't seem to be squaring-up for her. She wanted the umpire to do something before her whole game fell apart, thus the system.

"I want you to do something," she indicated to the umpire.

The umpire replied, "But, MISS CLARK, **HERE'S MY PROBLEM.**" The umpire had some problems and would cliché' these words throughout.

Well, everyone seemed to be having problems with this game and those problems didn't stop there either.

Marcia continued to explain. "Had we known the Dream Team was going to play this game with **AMBUSH TACTICS**, we would have been equipped."

As she continued to explain her plight, Ito contemplated.

Contemplation will prove to be a plus sign for the prosecution throughout this trial. Commentators were befuddled when Lance Ito passed the ball (game) back to the Head Hunters for a re-opening statement. They suggested that he had created a new ruling in the system—new case law for the game, they said. And this was more firewood, for the Dream Team to burn toward a repeal, if need be.

What a mess, also, for the sequestered jurors, long confined already, and perhaps now en-visioning their plight. How long could they be isolated like this and still retain a sense of sanity? What a mess—and it gets worse.

SECOND WEEK

(Monday, January 30, 1995)

To even the playing field, a hearing is held by the referee. It too was a window for the world to see and it seemed to make a difference in the Umpire's decisions.

Today, Orenthal's Dream Team gets a bad boy call—a lashing I should say. Lance Ito demonstrated his displeasure against the Dream Team, because of their surprise game play (a new witness list). You can't do that in the City of Angels, they were told.

The umpire/player discussions were held on new witness foul plays. Final analysis—defense player Cochran was given some community service duties. He was to complete his pitchers opening rounds to the jurors. But he was fined, so to speak, reprimanded, if you may. When he went back to finish his pitching duties, he renounced his old ways. He had a new body language—he was more reclined. He was more on the side of being somber in his pitches from the mound. Perhaps Ito's declaration was befitting the seriousness and nature of Cochran's foul play that he was charged with. I don't know.

This referee had been outraged, but was now inviting perhaps new—to this effect—case-law. The pundits speculated.

Alan Dershowitz, a celebrated appeals court lawyer and a Harvard Law Professor, was watching it all. Ito would now allow the Prosecution Team ten additional minutes to come back to the plate and restructure their game plan. Marcia had won another round.

(January 31, 1995)

The games would be put on hold again when testimony was presented on how Nicole, Orenthal's now-deceased ex-wife, had collapsed in the arms of Detective, Mike Farrell. She had been "hysterical and shaking," was the given testimony by Farrell, the 1989 investigating officer. Nicole had allegedly been abused by Orenthal on that night.

Prosecutors methodically opened this inning against the Dream Team recounting physical and mental abuse inflicted on the ex-wife by Orenthal.

(February 1, 1995)

When Head Hunter Darden took the pitcher's mound on a Dream Team play issue, pundit TV Commentators believed he too was treading on appeal ground. This issue of dreams was way out in left field. For the facts, this issue was out of the ball park. If a Defense team player should become ousted from presenting this type of game play again, experts knew and commentators were sure, this decision would come back to haunt THE PEOPLES court, in appeal. Dershowitz continued watching.

Here is what happened. A thought-to-be cousin of Player Cochran, Ron Shipp, came up to the plate. He was a retired police officer who had been in conversation with the defendant—conversation during which Orenthal remarked about a dream he had. He said O.J. indicated he had a lot of dreams about killing her (Nicole). Expert commentators indicated, evidence of a dream allowed in a murder case could lead to a reversal. Count this one against Referee Ito. He had made a boo-boo in his play calling. He allowed fantasy testimony in.

No one really knows what dreams mean and there was no foundation to this imagination, this illusion. Experts say this was capricious and could not be considered evidence—that dreams are nothing more than fantasies.

Ronald Shipp was also an "aspiring actor." He had a past alcohol problem and had considered himself a twenty-some year friend (perhaps foe) to Orenthal Simpson. Any future relationship between these two will be left to another history.

(February 2, 1995)

The Dream Team had sort of dropped the ball with Ron Shipp. As Carl Douglas, the hatchet man of the Dream Team, begged the referee for some relief on Ron's statement about the dreams, (which would be sure death to the defense). None was allowed. If it's going to be sure death, let's let it in, Umpire Ito indicated.

Head Hunter Marcia Clark was dressed to kill that day as this display of sentencing was handed to her team like a present. You could not help but notice her black attire. She was the undertaker—ready for the burial. The ball game was once again at low ebb for the Dream Team. Clark was all but laughing abdominally. She wanted to giggle—realizing the other team was now in a begging mode, and at her mercy. Right then she moved up to the plate, where Defense Douglas already was, and attempted to take his bat and knock him out of his box with it. But she wasn't able to.

Clark was her name, knocking home runs was really her game—about Twenty Five already. She's a real game winner, with few to no losses.

That's when Umpire Ito came to Douglas' rescue. He instructed him on how to hold his bat and how to swing on this play issue. It was then that Douglas stood up graciously for his teammates. He knocked a double. Some would call it a home run. All thanks to Referee Ito.

Here's another story on that play issue, concerning Ron Shipp. It seems that his past alcoholic rouse, his professionalism as a witness, all could perhaps demonstrate him to be a liar. His appearance of arrogance and personal opinion during cross examination did not help his credibility any either. He acted like a bit of a smart aleck toward the defense, and was clearly biased. This Head Hunter player, initially a credit, had turned out to be a lie-ability. The FACT, or FANTASY THEOREM, the DREAM testimony, all had been watered down—perhaps to naught. Shipp would be credited with a culprit's medal.

Several hits have been made, lots of errors, both teams have been left on, and lots of players are yet to come to bat. Ron Shipp had slithered back to the outfield and had now perhaps disenfranchised himself from his Twenty-Seven years (all be it lukewarm) friendship with Orenthal and his circle of friends. He had never played in this league before. Now, chances are, his opportunities have reached their limitations in the credibility department. Shipp's tryout had fallen short. Dream Team-er Carl Douglas, instead, became a star as he mutilated Shipp's opportunities to produce a positive effect as a favorable player for the Head Hunters team.

(February 3, 1995)

The games were a bit somber in early play today. Cheerless would be a sobering depiction of today's activities. The facts are cheerless for most every viewer. Nicole's sister, Denise Brown, tearfully described her sister's rocky relationship with the Heisman Trophy winner. It's puzzling, however, to harness proper ideology as to why Denise's testimonial, acts-and-plays, were a bit different from earlier game finesse. But, that doesn't really matter; we must take the high road on this media attitude. What matters in this thesis is that she was hurting from the loss of her loving sister.

As the author, I would like to take this time out, for me and the rest of the world to say, our hearts went out to Denise, her family and their circle of friends—and to Ron Goldman's' family and friends. We paused then to give our love and prayers. May God continue to bless you and yours in this uncalled for tragedy.

THIRD WEEK

(February 6, 1995)

Now, let us continue to look for lost balls, mishaps, and culprits.

What this inning had proven to viewers and spectators was that Orenthal when he imbibed was "a mean-drunkard." Alcohol drinking did not bring him joy. And Christopher Darden, this particular day, just didn't seem to understand the rules of the game of evidence. He, in a novice way, tried to garner an extra pitch with a picture photo. He wanted it in the game. This play was elementary and could have been devastating to the Head Hunters. Following that moment of insertion, the Dream Team could have asked for a mistrial. But, that was not anyone's intention. However, this game, with all of its cost, etc., could have been forced to become a play-over. This could have put an irreconcilable burden on the Prosecution. If this game had succumbed to the position of having to be played over, well . . . that could have surely put some jobs in jeopardy. Dershowitz was watching from a front row seat.

Shapiro, who had been set back somewhat on the teams line-up as a front line player and as a deal maker (now player manager), was back on the playing field once again today. He scored several needed points with his delicate handling of his world famous knuckle ball. He was throwing it at Nicole's sister, Denise, who had to be handled with kid gloves in all of these plays. By the time Shapiro had delivered all of his pitches, her alcohol drinking would prove to be a hindrance to her testimony; thus to the Prosecution's team. She was a recovering alcoholic. Her plays in today's game had changed the face of previous testimonial plays.

I think, however, that the biggest foul-play that started to be noticeable by many fans and foes alike—seemed clouded plays of Aldredism. Gloria Aldred, Denise's lawyer and a female activist, was having a driving force to bring down Orenthal (Orenthal the person), at all costs. Perhaps Denise had been prepped by this ideology. Perhaps several game players had been prepped in her fashion, as to Aldredism synonymity and her act of plays. We don't know, but Gloria seemingly had decided that if her group of folks were going to bring down Orenthalism and his type—this sort of male ideology, this sort of man, this act of misbehavior—they had better take advantage of this opportunity.

Perhaps, this thinking was apropos, but in a homicide? No! It would be proper to get—and with surety—the right culprit for the crime. Gloria, as a lawyer, should have known that there were specific rules to follow—that's the way it's done.

Aldredism had begun to take on a noticeable course of action on Ito's playing field. Some players were noticed batting with similar batting styles—different from before, and with different bats. Take down another point from the Society. It didn't need this course of action. Charge it to Aldredism.

Giggles could be heard broad and wide, as well as in Ito Parks and Fields, when Cochran, with a father's mentality, told Umpire Ito that he would deal with Head Hunter Chris Darden later. He was responding to Darden's remarks that his self adopted Step-Father, Johnnie Cochran, was picking on him. He wished openly to Umpire Lance Ito that he would stop Cochran from picking on him—said with a playful smile, of course. And why not, it all seemed to be just a game.

(February 7, 1995)

Tia Gavin, a Mezzaluna Restaurant employee marked a new show of play for the Head Hunters. Marcia Clark, gracefully, strode up to the podium. She had been analyzing her strategy from a sideline vantage point. She had been giving Darden some exposure and playing time before entry into the ruffian segment of the series. It was a sure thing that some players would drop out of the line-up before the final shot was fired.

As in the Medieval Period, when games had Champions, Head Hunter Clark was truly a

Champion for her subjects. She really is a Star, you know, and we all enjoy watching her performances. She's smart, almost heady (perhaps headstrong). She is respectfully coquettish (with a feminine temperament), self assured and has a single mind in this game; that is, to win. She's a team player and doesn't hog publicity. She can take it or leave it. She will have to take it during this battle, as the media finds her irresistibly magnetic.

Ron Goldman's time line was established today. He had catered to the ill-fated tragedy of the mothers' glasses by going back to Bundy, the scene of the homicide—the scene of the opening play of these games.

By the end of the day Clark would come under fire from Cochran. He had noticed her wearing an angel's pin—just as Denise had worn the day before. To Cochran's dismay, this was a demonstration to him of more Aldredism. He made her take it off and told her not to wear it back in HIS court room, never again. We haven't seen it since.

Marcia is some lady. When Cochran asks her to do a thing and he ask her in a proper manner, she will more than likely accommodate him in this trail—especially when Ito signals such a motion to the affirmative.

(February 8, 1995)

An outside player, Counselor Carl Jones, attempted to quash Simpson's first wife, Marguerite Simpson-Thomas', subpoena. A strong argument was held to the referee to stand up and do his job. "Play the game right," he indicated. "You have the authority to call this play, Ref," Jones admonished. "I don't see any advantage to introducing this new player. I don't want her in this arena if I can help it. This player has no responsibility to an ill-served injunction."

His motion was strong, but it was denied. Simpson-Thomas will surely be a hostile witness for the Head Hunters. This could be a turning point in these games.

Eva Stein, Nicole's neighbor, was awakened from the persistent and annoyingly intense sound of Nicole's dog wailing. This was the night of the homicide. Eva was on display for possible stardom. I really don't think this was her cup of tea, but she had to be there.

Louis Karpf, Eva's boyfriend, was much like her. He wasn't looking for fame and fortune in this game either. The tune he played started to become garbled when the Head Hunters did not leave well enough alone in their direct examination. Cochran, who is also a professional sifter, sifted through some few ambiguities with Karpf.

Steven Schwab sought no fame either. He was another neighbor to Nicole. He testified that Nicole's dog had blood on its paws. He had been out walking his dog.

No one is sure which day the famed dog, KATO, will take the stand and tell the whole story from a dog's point-of-view. Science is saying this technology will be a matter of time. As you might know, time should be of little or no consequence in the case of these series. Prosecution was reserved in calling KATO (the dog as he had been referred) to the stand as late as need be. I thought, these games may never end.

(February 9, 1995)

Today's games include Marcia Clark throwing some friendly balls at the officer who arrived on the crime scene first. Officer Robert Riske indicated that this part of his professional experience had been on-the-job training. He had been ill-trained, for his part in the first scene of the homicide, back on June 12, 1994.

He testified in the courtroom he saw a letter with Simpson's name on it, the un-melted ice cream, etc., etc., and all but Hades broke loose. Orenthal somehow had been involved, the officer seemed to expose. When he let these mice out of his trap, I knew, somehow, the defense would have a field day on this issue. That's just what they did.

Cochran, at the plate, continued to hurl little, significant darts and holes into the Prosecutions game, through Officer Riske. Riske, beginning to be a risk for the Head Hunters, was showing indications of some dishonesty about Mark Fuhrman's time line whereabouts.

It was getting late in the evening and Clark was beginning to squirm. Darden was on the edge of his seat, while Hodgeman was re-thinking his move back onto the playing field. Then there was a call for another timeout at side-bar. They had been there hundreds of times before; another trip seemed routine.

Cochran told Ito that Head Hunter Clark could explain away and at the end of these games she would still probably be explaining.

Somehow Umpire Ito always demonstrated a leaning Tower of Pisa in favor of the Prosecutors. He had been one himself, after all. This **LEANING TOWER OF PISA** was no different. But, Ito is a man of great wisdom. He always finds virtuous reasoning in his explanation of equity.

We are perhaps a minor fraction through this circus. The tell-tale signs have started to lead us toward acts of mean-spiritedness on both teams. Stay tuned for next Tuesday. Both teams have a bye scheduled for Friday and Monday. Monday is President's Day. Viewers are starting to seer and jeer, t-h-e-a-t-e-r, theater. That's just what many are saying; it's mostly, all theater—a show. Public lynchings are better off humanized with swift blows. Caning was really unnecessary; if we honestly believed a person was innocent until proven guilty. They say it's the law. I said structure the games properly, be democratic, but let's get this marathon on the road before winter sets in again. When all the scores are in, decide decisively and move on. I think that should be the active law.

As Lance Ito would say, "HERE'S THE PROBLEM" . . . Some of us would like to get back to All MY CHILDREN, A GUIDING LIGHT, LOVING, AND PERHAPS ANOTHER WORLD. SOME OF US ARE BORED WITH THIS GLOBAL EXCITEMENT.

FOURTH WEEK

(February 12, 1995)

All caravans and players were put on notice today being Sunday, that all playing and game sites were typically back in session.

(February 14, 1995)

The second officer to arrive on the scene was Sergeant David Rossi. Rossi was a fifteen-year veteran. He took the stand and said he had arrived on the scene at 12:25 A.M. There was a slight miscalculation; other testimony had indicated a five minute difference—12:20 A.M. Time was making a difference in having a winning edge in this game-of-sorts.

Clark was throwing some soft pitches to Rossi in a tit-for-tat rhetorical relay production. But there was no real drama in this friendly conference. Rossi was simply verifying much of Riske's story, before him—not all, but most of his story.

F. Lee Bailey, the famed player of the Dream Team, was churning the calm emotions of Sgt.

Rossi. Viewers and listeners were gathering their thoughts and hanging on to their chairs for the fireworks to come. Analyzers had been computing their arithmetic. Players on each team were adding and subtracting their scores and so were the commentators. The system and its players were in full gear. They were all racing their motors, and each were about to blow their head-gaskets.

Bailey threw few to no soft balls to Rossi. Instead, he barraged Rossi with rapid fire-balls. They were very effective, especially for theater. Rossi begin to appear edgy. Even Umpire Ito was asking for a time-out

Perhaps he needed time to square up his **LEANING TOWER OF PISA**—for an appearance toward fair play. He seemed to lean one way most of the time. His spouse has an office in the rival team's court—you should know.

A SOCIETY GONE AWRY, Colin Ferguson, the Long Island train slaughterer; was his folly that of an American atypical, or a CERTAIN psychopath? And are both his and Simpson's trial akin to the status quo we live with in America? Who Knows? Here is the update on the Ferguson media rival. **THE NEWS REEL** . . . .

On the other side of the country as we take a brief look at the case of **Colin Ferguson**, who was holding court also. **The Long Island, New York,** train slayer—was he a crazy lunatic or what? Or did he just want to have his day in court? He was performing his own lawyering. Many were puzzled about the rules of that game—about their system, about their media. Some watchful eyes had moved past being perplexed with that series. They were now looking for the proper rhetoric to sanitize their act and those responsible persons, who had let that game out of its cage.

The Eastern Courts with Colin Ferguson will probably never compete with the Orenthal Western Courts, not in capital competition anyway. But, somehow, each of these courts and their games have already met their match in substance, in detail and in the media frenzy. Both had already gone too far. Someone indicated, these courts had been synergistically forced into a new paradigm by Americanized paranoia. Both cases had been collaborative models—with auras of courtroom disorders—perhaps typical American mayhem these days.

Susan Smith, (who had drowned her two youngsters in the river) was also having try-out trials. My heart cries for her predicament. I would never reference her to **BEAUTY AND THE BEAST**. God will forgive those who have made this analogy—if they ask.

(February 15, 1995)

Rung hung and strung out to dry. That was the appearance of the Head Hunter's game today—and with F. Lee Bailey's cross examination.

Marcia Clark re-directed, but the jurors will have to discuss this inning among themselves—about the issues, that is. Rossi, the person in charge of securing the area at Bundy, was being persecuted into a predicament by Bailey. How will that play out to the jurors? I'm not sure.

But, fifteen years ago Rossi had read completely the manual that designated most all of his duties as a sargeant; he had only read it in sections since. By the time Bailey had finished throwing hard balls at Rossi's head, besides stringing him out to dry, there were questions left in various minds. Questions about what else Sgt. Rossi should have done in properly securing this homicide scene. As I said before, this call will ultimately be left to the jurors in their final notions, or is it motions?

Detective Ron Phillips, an officer for twenty eight years and a partner to Mark Fuhrman for approximately four years, came up to the batting box.

Clarence G. Hanley

(February 16, 1995)

Pitches and catches with Ron Phillips continued between he and Head Hunter Marcia Clark. Not much excitement, yet. There was little to no explosions in today's games with the prosecutors.

Outside the gates at Ito Fields, the news media was stirring up some commotion with innuendoes. Commentators were prophesying with their TV questionnaires and their writing pads. It seemed very hard for viewers to do any personal and intelligent thinking on their own; the media had been doing that for them. Those media buffs have to be getting big bucks for their continued service; they never quit.

Word by word, analysis could be found on most every TV station and otherwise.

They were explaining the ramifications of each splinter in the player's bats, how round the game ball should be, and what the ball park audiences and players could and should expect.

With a stroke of their lens-and-pens, or utterances of their questioning voices, wherever and whenever directed, syllables, Grammatik and syntaxes were being checked. Respondents were being given one more willing chance. Others were being offered reluctance. Media was resting on their first amendment and probably never notices the problems they were perpetuating. Sounds silly? It is. Press, media and analysis—all perhaps should have gotten together early on and told us how these games would play out. Then we would not have to follow the daily routine of it all.

We could hardly enjoy the plays, or any of the innings. Press, media and analysis pundits—all had beguiled our notions away from anticipation—or was it the other way around?

Oops! I was watching TV just now. Ito has made a few uncalled-for pitches for Head Hunter Clark. She bungled a few of her balls. She was throwing at Ron Phillips. Ito jumped in with a few correctional tosses, to help keep Clark on course with her follow through. What a coach! And, of course, referees are players too. Ito is.

When Cochran started his round, he seemed to be interested in how well Phillips understood the playbook—just like he did with Rossi. He wanted to know from Ron Phillips if he understood all the plays. He wanted to know why he had deviated from previous plays. Was it because of current circumstance?

Subjects, spectators and onlookers who had chosen the Dream Team as their champions were mostly proud of Cochran's performance this day. He prodded and pushed, negotiated and speculated. He would smile, and then he would get serious, very serious. He showed and then he would tell. I think it's fair to say his subjects were very pleased.

Others were awed. He made the color-blind color focused.

Cochran put a jacket back on Phillips' partner, Fuhrman, where he had previously indicated there was none—that he never wore a jacket. Cochran's performance was nothing short of spectacular. When he had finished with this inning, lawyers everywhere were taking notes. Commentators had revived their forecasts and the Head Hunters were left in dismay—once again.

The world's greatest female Head Hunter, Marcia Clark, will come back for more in re-direct. But, as I said before, if you were a subject of the Dream Team, any direct or re-direct would only have been null, devoid and vilified this day, because of Cochran's star like performance.

(February 17, 1995)

Cochran continues to pound away at Phillips.

There has to be a degree of great respect awarded Ron Phillips—mainly because of his lack of arrogance. The position he was in could have given him every right to appear arrogant—say . . . like Ron Shipp. He wasn't. He seemed helpful and honest, even when he had to admit he'd fallen short of his full duties as a seasoned officer of the law. He simply indicated that he didn't always do his job.

One time today when Clark objected to Cochran's cross exam, Cochran indicated, no! He told Ito, just let me talk to Miss Clark. He took her aside field and explained a few points to her. She laughed and smiled sociably, turned and indicated to Ito that she was okay now. Cochran proceeded.

Subjects who were concerned for their champions were questioning, where's the war? Let's get it on! This is no way to play chess. There's no competition here! Too many mutual agreements! Well . . . maybe not. Marcia knows her law and for sure she knows exactly what she's doing. Stay tuned for hardball on this one and let's sees what happens later on. Surely, the defense has to fear that old adage: "Hell hath no fury like a woman scorned."

Det. Tom Lange, sometimes called Frederick, was a member of the LAPD since 1968. He has been a detective for twenty-one years. He is not a rookie, and in many ways he needs to make a good showing, in order to succeed as a favorable player on the Prosecution's team. We will see how well he does during his tryout. But, before the week will come to an end, let us first check in with Ms Clark.

Marcia Clark wants to introduce new playing gear, a glove and cap, before the close of conference today. These items were not necessarily the kind of gear today's baseball players would normally use in their regular games. They should be used as play-off togs. Anyway, I think this glove was one of the homicide items and so was the cap. It was a knitted sock cap. We'll seek the details on those items as information becomes available.

Also, the Head Hunters will soon be moving into mid-season with a new lineup and other new playing materials. DNA will be a new area for these games

It appears that future games will be very competitive. Just remember, there will evolve many forces between two wills, forces between two evils, forces between two teams and forces between two sides. I'm not un-sure about proper subtitles for these teams and players. But, one can be sure, that will all play itself out in time.

Three days will pass before players will come back to Ito Fields. Today is Friday and Monday is President's Day. We resume on Tuesday.

Here is a projected line-up of coming attractions. Many pundits think the Dream Team Defense Machine will schedule its world renowned FAST BALL pitcher, F. Lee Bailey, against the clever BAT of Mark Fuhrman. This should prove to be a tug of war and matrimony of wills.

FIFTH WEEK

(February 21, 1995)

Counselor Carl Jones came back to Ito Fields in support of Mrs. Rosa Lopez. This was the lady star who wanted to play on Orenthal's team. It seems Mrs. Lopez was lost and now she was found. They thought she had gone back to South America, (El Salvador). That was not true. She was found by the news media in Los Angeles.

They had been ribbing Mrs. Lopez about whether or not she was going to try out for the Dream Team. At this time, she was asking to be left alone. But they couldn't do that—that would mean PEACE. This was WAR—WAR between the press, WAR between the tubes and WAR between the media. All were taking no prisoners.

Head Hunter Darden was in denial of this Dream Team player being examined for the league, or even trying out for a spot, especially outside of Ito Fields (perhaps on video tape).

This was when F. Lee Bailey made an analogous perception. He asked Referee Lance Ito if the courts could show leniency on behalf of an animal (as a witness) through it's time of wailing, would the courts be willing to allow leniency on behalf of a human person, a neighbor. She, who is willing to testify in behalf of seeing Orenthal's Bronco at a previously stated designation,

With an argument like that Ito agrees to consider the issues at hand with a conditional exam. This will protect all involved. An in-video testimony will be taken outside of regular court.

A few negative choices of remarks became a bit of cross fire between Darden and Jones, with Bailey trying to take up the slack. Ito told each one of them to shut up and sit down.

Detective Tom Lange was brought back to the batting box for more direct pitches. This was kind of like being at the carnival, or a circus, or perhaps an amusement park. Remember how and when you threw the ball at a subject and if you hit the center ring, the seat dropped and the subject fell—into a tub of water? Lange, who is a very dull player, but a very meticulous teammate for the prosecution, fell into this tub of water several times. He was trying to do a good job playing team-ball with the Head Hunters. It wasn't working. He created a problem for the Prosecutor's entire series.

These games haven't had much shifting, thus far. But there is starting to be some motion. I can see the wave a-comin—'comin around the bend.'

Referee Lance Ito seems to have little to no patience demonstrating his dislike for female posturing. He doesn't seem to like that sort of ball playing. In such cases, he seems to lend favor to the Dream Team—usually favoring Cochran. That will prove to be a front.

(February 22, 1995)

The Dream Team is seeking to undermine all of the prosecutor's plays, balls, and errors. They are now backing into their offensive mode to do that. They are continuing to go against Det. Tom Lange in cross examination, pitching almost all strikes at his bat.

It might be clearer to note that this segment of these games holds the appearance of a tug-of-war but with some civility (only some).

Tom Lange has gone against Referee Ito's rules, not to watch TV about testimony. He has clearly done this. Instead of Cochran stopping his cross exam of Lange and going to side-bar to have his testimony thrown out, he doesn't. He simply continued to degrade, ridicule and demolish Lange's particular department, his policemen and his entire game. This was designed to demonstrate to the jurors the true credibility of the LAPD. This department had not taken finger prints or blood samples from the back gate of the scene. They had not taken blood trace evidence from the deceased's fingers or back, nor had they handled the entire scene in a way indicative to the crime. Thus, the charges that they had practiced and played by were done badly and now seemed true—and these were the tell-tale signs.

Cross exams against Lange caused him to foul his ball too many times, before striking out. Of course, this doesn't quite lose ones entire game for their team, but it doesn't help your team win either. Lange hadn't helped very much.

It should be noted that Lange was one of the older, less agile players. Sometimes he seemed to be playing with a forced memory loss—nothing like the latter-day players (or is it saints?). Anyway, he was forgetting some crucial and decisive plays. You cannot do that—not in this game for sure.

Also, no team should expect to win without their top-of-the-line plays, players and equipment. The fans of Los Angeles thought they had fully financed their players, i.e. team. But this was not the first time an LAPD team had bungled their game. This just seemed to be a repeat, and equipment might only be a portion of all that they would need in these play offs.

All of these things were starting to take their toll toward **IMPORTANCE, SIGNIFICANCE and CONSEQUENCE**. It has always been noted that, if you are going to have a winning team, each player has to be playing in unison with the others. The

Dream Team had most of the prosecution's team confused.

The repetitive litany of **RUSH TO JUDGEMENT**, was now, more than ever, becoming an original habitat to Lange's police department. Faulty testimony was surfacing, as the Defense continued to home in on Lange's not-so-helpful testimony for the prosecution. What can we expect next?

(February 23, 1995)

It is Det. Tom Lange's fourth day. He remains under fire by Cochran of the Dream Team. As to how many bullets he will digest, we will soon see.

Each side will now argue a new video tape. This tape will show a distant view of the people's side. All of them are walking through the scene. The defense wants to argue about the many players who are improperly walking on the playing-court at Bundy. Up 'til now, there had been only a few explosions from either side, and Ito's wisdom on entry of the video tape was a split decision but set for a time bomb.

Hold on! An explosion just erupted at Ito Parks and Fields. It seems Christopher Darden just BLEW UP.

Somehow, the Dream Team has confused the Head Hunters (a part of their strategy). They've forced Prosecutor's team-player, Christopher

Darden, to pull his FAILSAFE BUTTON. That's when all of his rockets went off, sky-high, and the ball park lit up like the Fourth of July.

Umpire Ito had to cite Darden for contempt. He had been verbal, hot headed, and had made a negative exchange with the umpire. He had been provoked by a sly remark from Johnnie Cochran. Even I know better, and I am not an attorney—you must respect the umpire's territory. For that matter, one has to respect another's home. Darden had not adhered to Ito's Empire; he had been given specific directions. Such problems with Darden were visible to many spectators now, as it had been earlier in these games.

The Umpire called for a recess. The question now is . . . will Head Hunter Darden apologize to the head personage of these games, or does he think he can take his toys and rally on home. I don't think so.

At this very moment everyone was waiting to see what his next act will be. Ito, by now, was offering Darden three chances to apologize. But why three chance? Right . . . It's a game—a baseball game. Its three strikes then you're out.

Darden was now asking for an independent counselor, indicating he wanted to challenge the uno-uno corporate persona of these games.

Ito, once again, informed Darden, "there are two issues on the table to be disposed of—apologize or else." (The words were like a gunfighter's shootout.) 'Else' meant, he would probably be taken into civil custody. Darden was in denial and perhaps thought he was entrenched in a WW II JAPANESE CONFLICT.

But he was ready for battle. He, evidently, thought he had spent too many years in grad school to be taken prisoner by this enemy, especially without an intelligent fight to the BAR. Some viewers actually did think he was drunk. The BAR, I suppose, had something to do with his unwillingness to act soberly. He wanted to take this up with his association. Everyone knew that this was Ito's property and he was assumed by law to be trespassing. He was in violation; everybody knew that—except him.

Darden made several body twists, did some head exercises, made a few hand movements, tried to smirk a smile before Clark suggested some of her first aid, (counseling support for him vs. Ito's wrath).

Ito didn't buy her act. But, in an effort not to be as heavy-handed with his bat as he could have been—with such an unseasoned act-without-contrition—he proceeded with the following. He asked each of them to come to the EMPIRE'S dugout (side-bar). It was at side-bar that William Hodgeman rushed back to the playing field to remind Darden that it was best to continue to play ball—which this was no time for pouting, hospitalization or jail. Just look at me, I'm out for the season, he wanted to say. He stated, "Quite honestly, Man, it's not worth it. Just go back and play your best game. Stay cool, brother. My people are with you." **Gave him a jive handshake and backed off.**

Darden didn't seem to understand the rules of this game, nor Hodgeman's brother rhetoric. He really wanted to take his equipment, all of his balls, and just go home. He wanted to quit. But, finally, after twisting and turning a few more times and finally muscling himself up to the podium deck, he did what was expected. But it took some effort. He tried once, twice and finally he made a forced effort and a reluctant apology. Ito reciprocated—with an apology of his own—back to Darden.

Mark your score sheets . . . two players down for the Head Hunters and several plays left to go.

Hang in there, Marcia Clark; the men are going down—all of them. Your men will need your stamina, as well as your wisdom to keep pace.

Cochran took the field again, having put aside earlier fallouts caused by penalties. This time, when he took his field position, it was more like going to a firing range. This game had just seen fireworks and both sides seemed to have been firing real bullets—big ones. No one got killed, but the Head Hunters have been badly damaged. Their casualty numbers were mounting enormously—even outside of Ito Parks and Fields.

Earlier today, Gil Garcetti, the head honcho prosecutor, conceded in a public announcement that if his side lost, with all of their efforts, he would ask for a rematch. When I heard this, I realized this justice rhetoric had somehow gotten lost underneath American standards and was being replaced with WINNING AT ALL COST. Shapiro rebutted Garcetti's response—(in the news media, of course). He said, "Prosecution must have had very little to no evidentiary strength for them to give up so soon—having claimed they had so much. Didn't they know we just started these games and it's entirely too soon to concede. We want them to give us our chance to put on our case and to play our game—our way."

(February 25, 1995)

Both teams held a conference today, in the presence of the umpire. The Prosecutors are in support of Mark Fuhrman's rights. The Dream Team is in support of Orenthal's rights. The N-Word was at the center of these hearings, but defense also wanted to hear taped testimony from Rosa Lopez.

Cheri Lewis was asking Ito to leave out negative information about Fuhrman. She wanted any and all testimony against him to be unimpeachable.

Rosa Lopez was waiting in the rear to be heard—on camera. She was the person who saw Orenthal's Bronco parked at his home at the time of the homicide.

F. Lee Bailey argued that this was not a unique case with Lopez. His proposal was not to paint or taint the witness (Mark Fuhrman) with an undeserved accusation. He further indicated that respectable counsel should only ask questions that they could lawfully back up. If they should attempt to go beyond this latitude, they should be handled with the heavy hand of THE GREAT EMPIRE OF LANCE ITO.

F. Lee Bailey's suggestion will stand. Cochran asked Ito about wanting to proceed with Rosa Lopez. She will be leaving for El Salvador tomorrow. She is trying to escape the hoopla of the media. Cochran wants to interview her outside the view of cameras.

Cochran, in an evidential hearing of Lopez, reported that she was tired of not being left alone. She could not go anywhere and her daughter was going to put her out—mostly because she was going to testify. Also, she indicated that her son had died, which was another problem for her. She had business back home in El Salvador to take care of.

Darden was anxious to rib Rosa Lopez. He did, and he was a bit ugly with her. He called this witness, this public servant and doer of duty, a liar. Some will not like that language. It was thought he might lose credibility points. We'll have to wait and see.

Hold on, fans. Rosa Lopez has been found in three truth shortcomings—perhaps lies. She had made a prior reservation; her sister may not be sick, currently. (Lopez hadn't talked to her sister in a month or so); and she didn't seem to have a dislike for the news media. She told one newscaster that she really loved the work she did and also mentioned in court, that the media could follow her to buy her ticket, if they didn't believe she was going to El Salvador.

*   *   *

JOHNNIE . . . JOHNNIE . . .
JOHNNIE COCHRAN

WHAT CAN YOU EXPECT FROM YOUR FANS?

YOUR BATS GONE FLAT, YOUR HURL HAS
CURLED

GOING SOUTH, IS ONE OF YOUR ALIBI GIRLS

AFTER THIS, ONE HUNDRED AND EIGHTY
DEGREES TURN

SUBJECTS ARE NOW CONCERNED ABOUT
THE DOUGH YOU'LL EARN

*   *   *

We will find out what happens when everyone returns to Ito Parks and Fields.

Here is what transpired. Lopez' credibility wasn't getting any better during Darden's cross—examination. When he had finished with her, she had been cooked—well-done.

Cochran sought to re-establish and restore Lopez' credibility. It seems she did actually have a reservation to another state. From there she was expected to fly to El Salvador.

Her credibility earlier had gone awry—with lies and contradictions it seemed—but maybe not.

Zulem Lida, the travel agent, had retrieved Rosa Lopez' credibility considerably. Torn asunder, confused, afraid and with some realization of the possibilities—by Referee Ito—she was left afraid and in a waiting mode.

Darden will accept admission of the Lopez conditional examination—but first, another coffee break—for everyone.

SIXTH WEEK

(February 27, 1995)

This trial once again bordered on derailment. It seems that Rosa Lopez and various Spanish idioms, i.e., El Salvadorian versus Mexican colloquialism, have their differences. She could not understand all of the words put to her by her translator—at least not in all their forms and fashions. So, although syntax and Grammatik were basically the same in her language, the courts wisely suggested a certified interpreter from El Salvador.

New information! Over the weekend, the prosecution is now changing their agreement to the court. They decided they will need to research Rosa Lopez further, in order to comfortably cross examine her story. Lopez' testimony would be out of turn; that also would be a problem for the prosecution.

On another front, the Defense is perhaps left to a one-sided hearing. Prosecutor Marcia Clark indicated it would probably be March before the Prosecution could intelligently cross-examine Lopez. Marcia realized that taking her complete testimony would hand-cuff the people's rights to a fair trial, if taken out of order.

The Defense was livid. They argued differently, as you would expect, but to no avail. Lopez' testimony will be taken by video, but does not limit prosecution to further research.

Guess what! A **MYSTERY VIDEO TAPE** has arisen and this little present to the Prosecution doesn't look good for the Defense. Rosa Lopez had given an interview on this tape several months ago.

But, it appears some issues might not pair up. Defense's disregard and non-disclosure of the tape-in-question, to the Prosecution, will be penalized for this misact of conduct. Also, it is believed by Prosecution that Rosa is a liar. Is Rosa Lopez a liar against, or a savior for, the Dream Team Defense Machine? Inquiring minds want to know. Stay tuned as we proceed tomorrow.

(February 28, 1995)

Both sides will be provided with investigator Bill Pavoloc's taped transcript of Rosa Lopez's statement back in July, 1994. Ito suspected there was a second tape. However, Pavoloc didn't have another tape nor did he have any additional notes in his possession. He had promised the court he would check his records the day before.

Everyone watching these games was confused as to whether, this tape from the Defense's side was a material omission, or otherwise. After the rigmarole and some clearing of smoke (my God, there was so much smoke). Anyway, Ito took Cochran's suggestion—to require the prosecution to listen to the twelve minute (fifteen minute) tape over their lunch period. Cochran also asked that he be able to continue with his cross of Rosa Lopez. We are waiting for that answer.

Ito has given an extra half hour for lunch on behalf of the Prosecution. About the mishandling of the tape in-question: It seems the genius of the Defense has saved them once again from the woes of Referee Lance Ito, who could have shackled them with sanctions. The appearance of this tape was late, very late—as far as discovery rules were concerned. Both sides have been scarred with these same woes, but the Defense has currently taken this (negative limelight to hand) and it doesn't look very good for their strategy. Their genius came with their fall-guy. A fall-guy for the Defense came forward, via telephone, to admit he had been the problem. He confessed that he had not made this taped information known or available to his client, Orenthal's defense team. The investigator's procedure in passing on reports to a client was usually by transcripts. In this case, the tape was made in the absence of a witness. Otherwise, the testimony would have been transcribed, as usual.

Since Referee Ito had bellowed p-l-a-y b-a-l-l, way back, and well over a month ago, there just has not been much ball playing. Many spectators

Clarence G. Hanley

are wondering if this is the way the games are played. Is this the way our system works, or is this the way of posturing, in an effort to prove the systems net worth? Others suspect that the referee has not been the most forceful role-model in keeping these games forthright and fancy free. Viewers really wanted this court to get this show on the road. Many viewers were finding these weekly explosions disgusting. But, annoyed as they may be, they also know that it's the same music that keeps them and millions of others humming along with (Mitch Miller's) immortal tunes. Like each of these millions, reluctantly they're singing . . . .

> *Take me out to the ball games,*
> *Take me out to the game.*
> *Buy me some candy and crackerjacks,*
> *I don't care if I ever get back.*
> *Let me root root root for the home team.*
> *If they don't win, it's a shame.*
> *'Cause it's one, two, three strikes you're out,*
> *At the old ball game.*

*　　*　　*

With seventy-five percent of this avid society and players on both sides of the spectrum, torn between the totem poles of race ideology, spousal abuse and the system, all sides are waving their flags in pursuit of personal justice. They realize it's the wrong arena, but it was the only game in town at the moment. So . . . each had gotten on this bandwagon and were riding their subtle jargons with great display.

I am only the announcer. But, I think, with me veering off the course of these games, the following might have a proper place. We'll turn our onward march back to the games after these messages.

Here it is. The subtle cantations promulgating through the crevices of American lifestyles are sometimes nonsensical incoherent verbiage. Many times it's all designed to put each of us behind the eight ball. The eight ball gets the attention, while important issues and other things fall into the pockets. That has always been an unfavorable position to be in for the rest of the billiards, (balls) or the players in these games. But, that's where we remain, that's where we are—in the pockets. We can't seem to get past that eight ball and it is no one's fault but our own—a thought to ponder.

What you have just pondered is, in fact, a simple analogy of our society, our justice system, our way of life. Some will not like that passage but some do not like the truth; it puts us behind the eight ball and that's not where we want to be. I really think we have to decide between two ideals: due process of the law, or due process of stage—as in, ALL THE WORLD IS A STAGE AND WE ARE JUST THE PLAYERS—sometimes being played upon. (SHAKESPEARE).

Meanwhile . . . let's get back to the games.

(March 1, 1995)

Replete and abound with starts and stops—rhetoric, sandbagging and posturing—we anxiously begin today's play with players hovering over the batter's plate, as in lawyer's podium and courtroom. While tension is not the motivating factor in these games, this game has plenty of it. Cochran wants to play ball—not that he hasn't been the reason for the stoppages—but he is ready to play with HIS balls of course. Neither team, with the jurors, will be taking the playing field until next week. The games will continue today with other argumentum delays.

What a series, THE ORENTHAL JAMES SIMPSON WORLD SERIES.

Gerald Uelman argues against Cheri Lewis not to have to turn over any and all of their incomplete reports per discovery, or otherwise. Ito will rule tomorrow evening.

Another juror was released, leaving fewer alternates.

(March 2, 1995)

The Dream Team, asking for relief from sanctions yesterday, was dreaming to think their sinister scheme would go without any reprimand. Marcia Clark intoned that a reprimand was in order, in the form of sanctions. She wanted the judge to tell the jurors what happened and to let her tell them again in her closing swing. She said, in effect, "Judge, they have been bad, but we are good." Ito then opined that the pendulum has been swinging both ways in these games, but fairness would be his forte—this time.

Both teams, and the system, remain in conference today. Darden rigorously cross examined Rosa Lopez. He was trying to establish her testimony and credibility as false, for a jury presentation. He seemed to be playing a good game, at the pitcher's mound. At the same time, he was looking like a time bomb waiting to explode. Of course his anxiety was promulgated by Cochran's several objections. Just stay tuned on this one. There's a soul match going on here—it has nothing to do with these games. Cochran has lit Darden's very short fuse—without a match I should say. We will have to wait and see if there are more fireworks on this issue.

WIRE REPORT . . . . Gordon Clark, Marcia Clark's ex-husband, is now asking for custody of their two boys. How timely! This is an outside play, but it may have a lot to do with the outcome of the ORENTHAL SERIES. We will bring you mini reports as they develop. Meanwhile, let us get back to Ito Parks and Fields.

Darden began to perform very well—after he had settled down. He was playing much better now. He wasn't swinging at just any 'old' ball. He was doing a good job on the pitcher's mound. Very unusual, but he was going on too long on this issue and was diluting his measures of successful testimony—repetition. He was keeping Lopez in the batting box too long. She's been getting used to his pitching style and is comparably batting in a style of her own. She continues to bat her balls all over the surface as a novice, but, quite honestly, some of her balls will score points. She never wavers from her central purpose—to say what she saw that single night shortly after Ten PM—Orenthal's Bronco.

Lopez doesn't have to be a good player for the Defense; they have many other good plays and players. But, it's possible; they could lose in spite of this player. She floats on troubled waters and now her sea of buoyancy is losing its tendency to remain afloat. Cochran, however, has the ability to recover the Dream Team from drowning.

IT'S ABOUT MONEY. Remember early on when I mentioned that the media must be making big bucks from this hurrah? Well, it seems that the ticket booth (prosecutor's side) is asking for a cut. They are now asking for part of Television and Newspaper receipts. Some are saying it's against California law—for media sharing, that is. Media indicated that the First Amendment protects and allows them every right to carpetbag this media pot-of-gold. Their forefathers saw to it that it would be there for their plucking, whenever the vegetation was ripe. And ripe it is, with this frenzy.

(March 3, 1995)

Darden, with Lopez, a little short of needed focus—continued in a kind of sing-song display, dealing with TIME questions. That the time testimony was centered a-round a dog, tea, clock, and church. But cross was starting to be a chore from the Prosecution. Darden had begun row-boating uphill. There seemed to be a guessing and a hoping expectation. He was losing ground as she continued to be . . . a novice, or a liar? In many ways, Darden helped Rosa retrieve some credibility and verify THE ALIBI, merely by harping at her. His means to an end—to circumvent her testimony—made her even more determined toward THE ALIBI. People see what they see. You might say that she stayed the course. She stayed with her first story—THE TIME SHE WALKED THE DOG.

Rosa Lopez' story, over all, was not very credible, rhetorically. But here's my thinking. Some games are played very differently than other games. If the Prosecution does not have a strong blood case, if Mark Fuhrman, or some other important prosecution witness, weaves and bobs, Rosa Lopez will look like a star.

Cochran and Douglas were sanctioned with fines to pay Rosa Lopez' hotel bill. Other fines are in the amount of Nine Hundred and Fifty Dollars, for each.

SEVENTH WEEK

(March 6, 1995)

Finally, we were back to courtroom action and a new player on the field. His testimony is being taken out of order. Mark Storfer, a close-by neighbor to Nicole, who lives near Bundy, gave testimony today. On the night of June Twelfth, he heard her dog barking. It was Ten Twenty Eight (actually Ten Twenty Three). His clock was five minutes fast. Prosecution is continuing to try to establish the homicide time line and nullification of four persons in the neighborhood during that time frame.

Cochran had a great opportunity to blow Prosecution's police witness arrival time line. He didn't—not yet anyway. Their time lines are not matching (Police's with Storfer's) per police arrival time. Storfer assures Cochran he did not see four persons from his vantage point. Prosecution feels if he didn't see them that should be strong testimony. Of course he only occasionally looked out his bedroom window.

Det. Tom Lange is back. Cochran seems a little rusty today. He's probably having a hard time dealing with last week's penalties and fines. He starts to hammer away at Lange, with vintage cross-exams.

He centered his questioning on drugs, and whether the LAPD had ever considered anyone else for this homicide.

There was one bomb scare, no real hits, no real runs and Lange remains left on—five days now.

(March 7, 1995)

Det. Tom Lange, viewing these games from his hot seat of testimony, continued with much of the same.

When Lange was asked about the size of the glove (he said they were extra large), was it a coincidence that at that moment Orenthal spontaneously put his hands underneath his table. This is food for thought from the media pundits.

Barry Sheck was very upset about Marcia Clark's conclusion about blood (DNA) evidence under Nicole's fingernails. He indicated that they had not completed their in-depth study yet. Clark's conclusion was that it was Nicole's own blood.

Fuhrman is being lined up for testimony. His lawyer refutes wrongdoing and any release of Fuhrman's Internal Affairs Files. He doesn't mind his personal files being admitted, but not the messy unkempt stuff. What's going on?

Patty Goldman, it seems, can verify the mysterious shopping list found in Ron Goldman's pocket. The defense wants to know how it got there. Patty was Ron's Stepmother. She seemed to have a most wonderful civil disposition and mannerism.

(March 8, 1995)

Some busy work was satisfied before either team took the field today—much to the favor of the Dream Team. The Defense, which considers Mark Fuhrman a **ROGUE COP** player, has been given the go-sign on subpoenaing his records. They will also have access to his Internal Affairs Files.

Two additional players are expected to try out for this game: ex-housekeepers Michelle Arburdon and Cathy Randa. The Head Hunters would like to get their hands on recent telephone records of both these prospects. Ito will make a ruling after he views their records in chambers. Zyona Fredman, on the fence regarding this same issue, could also be a player.

Michelle's and Cathy's personal attorneys, working pro bono (they were real lawyers), argued admirably on their behalf. Stephen Solomon, for Michelle, argued her rights to freedom of association and a citizen's rights to privacy. Melvyn Sacks indicated that every defense person subpoenaed should run for cover. This statement was promulgated in direct reference to an earlier statement by the Prosecution that all of Defense's witnesses were thieves, thugs, felons or drug users. He also asked for sanctions against the prosecution for giving short notices on their client's subpoenas. Ito will make a later ruling.

Lange's seventh mainstay testimony from his hot seat as a witness postulated that this homicide was a rage killing. Johnnie Cochran of the Dream Team countered, "Not so!" And, in his re-cross, Cochran seemed to have diffused any of Head Hunter Clark's gains.

First, Lange couldn't seem to remember hardly any information pertinent to the defense, whereas questions and answers had been smooth-sailing with Prosecution before. However, Cochran took center stage in setting the stage with Lange's deficiency in testimony and his homicide duties. He simply, piece by piece, demonstrated to Lange what he should have done as a professional. By lunch break everyone, pundits and all, were left to believe this really was a drug case—and Faye Resnick was at the helm of it all.

From Cochran's vantage point, it seemed Resnick had freebased, freeloaded, free booted and free loved until finally she wrote her book, which was frazzled with a frantic fray about O.J. Cochran contended this was a necklace slaying—a Columbian necktie homicide. Money was owed and Faye Resnick could have owed that money for unpaid drugs. The Defense would have you believe, her book became her cover; Denise and Ron the victims and Orenthal the scapegoat.

Some are asking, how many runs, how many hits, who's left on? Well, the truth of that matter is, all avid viewers are asking that same question. Both teams are putting up scores, but many are continuing to give odds to the Dream Team. Their batting averages have made few dips and valleys. But, in all actuality, this game remains in its infancy, and with a one sided presentation—the Prosecution's.

(March 9, 1995)

For some, as I know it is for *AN ODE TO SATIRE*, everything is off to a slow start today. Det. Tom Lange is in his eighth day on the witness testimonial hot seat. So, perhaps some plays on words and the coining of a few ideas will be the order of this day, until this game is geared-up and further on its way.

As you may already know by now, the Dream Team's Cochran is faithfully on a drug trail. He is referencing Faye Resnick's book about her ordeal with drugs (a best seller). Here's my take on that.

The Dream Team had spread massive possibilities throughout the empire and Fay Resnick was just another impressive proposal for them. So, how can they go wrong? If you throw a lot of mud on anyone's wall, some of it will stick. The notice, seems to be at this point, is to wish Mr. Fuhrman good health, and also Madame Faye Resnick. Life will never be the same for either, and they will probably discover that more fame sometimes carries less respect.

The pun of the **GREAT EMPIRE of LANCE ITO** is demonstrative in many ways akin to the **GREAT EMPIRE of GREEK MYTH and their CIVILIZATION**, especially when they were at their height of splendor. When the Greeks held their great games in their great arenas—much like that of Ito Parks and Fields—there were many great heroes.

History recollection of this great Greek Empire is centered on memories of **GREEK MYTHOLOGY (THE KINGDOM OF OLYMPUS)**. Zeus, Prometheus, Heracles, Aphrodite, Poseidon, Pandora and others, were all great heroes of mine as a youngster (each for a different reason). I don't have time and space to explain that idea fully, but I'll give a synopsis of each. You might draw your own 'conclusion in wit' from their matter-of-fact personalities. Mythology has always had a practical parallel in our society, so every story should have its mythology in comparison.

TAKING A BREAK FROM THE ORDINARY CONFLICTS OF NATURE

Since Adam and Eve, conflicts of all kind have been a part of human nature—the Iliad had been no different. We are simply a people of conflict.

The Iliad was sometimes referred to as the Song of Ilion or Song of Ilium. It is an epic poem in dactylic hexameters. This poem is traditionally attributed to Homer. The setting was during the Trojan War. It was the ten-year siege on the city of Troy by the Greeks. It tells of the battles and events during the weeks of a quarrel between King Agamemnon and the warrior Achilles.

Although the story covers only a few weeks in the final year of the war, the Iliad alludes too many of the Greek legends and conflicts about the siege; the earlier events; such as the gathering of warriors for the siege; the cause of the war; and related concerns that tended to appear near the beginning. The epic narrative takes up events and prophesied the future—such as Achilles' looming death; and the sack of Troy. When it reaches the end, the poem told more or less a complete tale of the Trojan War.

Along with the Homer's Odyssey, the Iliad is among the oldest works of Western literature of conflicts, and its written version is usually dated to around the eighth century BC. In the modern vulgate, the Iliad contains 15,693 lines; it is written in Homeric Greek and dialect. Following is simply my facsimile of a likeness to the people of its time of conflict as with the Iliad and the Odysseys.

A conflict needed to be settled and Ito was the choice of the day as judge and not jury. While not necessarily a likeness to each and every player in my story . . . I see similarities to their human displays—and also to my story of satire.

(FROM HOMER'S ILIAD AND THE ODYSSEY)

The following is from Wikipedia, the free encyclopedia

ZEUS; was the greatest gods at a time of conflict to be settled—**Judge Ito**.

In the ancient Greek religion, Zeus is the "Father of gods and men" who rules the Olympians of Mount Olympus as a father rules the family. He is the god of sky and thunder in Greek mythology.

The judgeship of Ito's office . . . is simply the power of a god over his children in my satire.

PROMETHEUS; *was punished by Zeus for having stolen fire from heaven—Mark Fuhrman.*

In Greek mythology, Prometheus is a Titan, the son of Iapetus and Clymene, and brother to Atlas.

He was a champion for mankind, known for his witty intelligence. He stole fire from Zeus

HERACLES; *was the most illustrious hero of Greek mythology—Orenthal Simpson.*

Heracles Ancient Greek: from "Hera", and born Alcaeus, a divine hero in Greek mythology, the son of Zeus and Alcmene. He was the greatest of the Greek heroes; Heracles capturing the Cretan bull.

APHRODITE; *was the goddess of love—Nicole.*

Aphrodite is the Greek goddess of love, beauty, pleasure, and procreation. Her Roman equivalent is the goddess Venus.

TROS; *presumed to have been killed by Achilles —Ronald.*

In Greek mythology, Tros was a ruler of Troy and the son of Erichthonius (daughter of the river god Simoeis) or of Ilus I, from whom he inherited the throne; a position of great distinction.

It was from Tros that the Dardanians were called Trojans and the land named the Troad.

POSEIDON; *was the god of troubled seas—Gil Gaecetti.*

Poseidon is one of the twelve Olympian deities of the pantheon in Greek mythology. His main domain is the ocean, and he is called the "God of the Sea". Additionally, he is referred to as "Earth-Shaker".

PANDORA; *was endowed by the gods with all the graces—Marcia Clark.*

In Greek mythology, Pandora, (Pandora's Box) released all the evils of mankind—although the particular evils, aside from plagues and diseases, are not specified in detail by Hesiod—leaving only Hope inside once she had closed it again.

THANATOS: *was the child of night—Chris Darden.*

In Greek mythology, Thanatos, "to die, be dying" was the daemon personification of death. He was a minor figure in Greek mythology, often referred to but rarely appearing in person.

JASON; *son of Zeus; he wooed Demeter and was killed by Zeus—William Hodgeman.*

Jason is a hero of Greek mythology who led the Argonauts.

CRATOS; *was the personification of force—Professor Uelmen.*

In Greek mythology, Kratos or Cratus (Ancient Greek: English translation: "strength") was the personification of strength and power.

ATLAS; *was the carrier of the sky—Shapiro.*

In Greek mythology, Atlas was the primordial Titan who supported the heavens.

APOLLO; *was god of the sun—F. Lee Bailey.*

Apollo is one of the most important and complex of the Olympian deities. Apollo has been variously recognized as a god of light and the sun, truth and prophecy, healing, plague, music, poetry, and more. Apollo is the son of Zeus and Leto.

ODYSSEUS; *was known for his cleverness, versatility and perseverance—Johnnie Cochran.*

Odysseus or Ulysses was the Greek king of Ithaca and the hero of Homer's epic poem the Odyssey. He is known by the epithet Odysseus, the Cunning. He is most famous for the ten eventful years he took to return home after the ten-year Trojan War and his famous Trojan horse trick.

ANTIPHUS; *was a friend of Odysseus—Carl Douglas.*

Antiphus, son of Aegyptius, was a Greek commander who sailed from Troy with Odysseus.

IPHITUS; *was a friend of Heracles—(A.C.) Cowlings.*

Iphitos was a descendant of Oxylus. During his search for the cattle, Iphitos met Odysseus in Messenia, befriended him, and gave Odysseus his father Eurytus's bow. Iphitus took Heracles's cattle, and was ultimately killed when Heracles, in a fit of madness, threw him off a wall in the city of Tiryns.

PHEMIUS; *was a bard in the illustrious palace—Kato Kaelin.*

In Homer's epic poem, the Odyssey, Phemius is an Ithacan poet who lives in the house while attempting persuasions . . . Towards the end of the story Odysseus instructs Phemius to perform . . .

(AS NEAR AS I CAN TELL, THIS HAS BEEN THE CARICATURE OF THE PANTHEON IN MYTHOLOGY AND IN PART IS TAKEN FROM WIKIPEDIA)

Patti Goldman—Ronald Goldman's stepmother—finally took the witness box in an effort to be a part of this game. Her batting average was of little significance. A shopping list was presented and accepted. Her tryout was equally the same.

The games today were crowded outside Ito Parks and Field more so than inside. This was **MARK FUHRMAN'S DAY**. He will have several, and there will be more massive crowds. Where there are crowds, there are uncalled-for happenings. That's an expectation.

Centurion Mark Fuhrman entered Ito's Parks and Fields much like a stalwart stallion. He was flanked by several armed guards of his own but, centurion he might be, I doubt his ancient army will enable protective services when he meets the likes of the Dream Team. F. Lee Bailey will be firing cannonballs at his head. Lange, previously, had spent almost eight days embattled. But Fuhrman is expected to try to ward off Armageddon, in a fight against the **RACE CARD**, for as many days or more. Antagonisms will forefront defensive play, after Prosecution's direct.

In either event this game hopefully will play out its true meaning of the Constitution. But, when all is said and done, Fuhrman will surely proclaim, **"FREE AT LAST, FREE AT LAST, THANK GOD**

ALMIGHTY, I'M FREE AT LAST;" that is . . . to go to Idaho. They like him up there.

Will he have a sobering outcome? I doubt it. Will he be unscathed? I doubt that too. Will he be scarred? Unequivocally, yes! In fact, most all of these witnesses will be scarred—for life. This is the ORENTHAL SERIES, what can one expect. It's a ball game (a baseball game, a game of sports), played out of season, without a contract. Most players in the major leagues are now bewildered. The minors have hopes and are realizing their opportunities, but they will steer free also. However, that won't stop the dreamers, the want-a-bees. They are each buzzing the hive. They want to be players, on the inside, in the majors.

It had been smooth sailing for Mark Fuhrman with Marcia Clark's direction, by days end.

(March 10, 1995)

Day two, with Mark Fuhrman, is expected to coast smoothly for the Head Hunters. They are mostly directing their play toward future expectations. The Dream Team Defense Machine's super player, F. Lee Bailey, is waiting spitefully in the bullpen, I mean dugout. Bailey catapulted to fame back in the Sixties, when he reversed the conviction of accused wife-killer, Dr. Sam Sheppard, whose case was the inspiration for the famed series, THE FUGITIVE. He is expected to do well again.

Head Hunter Clark pitched a full set of innings with no hits, no runs, no fouls and no interruptions from the Defense's F. Lee Bailey.

There is an adjournment, with much left the same, until Monday. Clark remains in the pitcher's box, throwing homemade pitches—soft and easy.

EIGHTH WEEK

(March 13, 1995)

F. Lee Bailey, in discovery, argued so very eloquently without the ears of jurors. He wanted more of Fuhrman's testimony let in. Marcia Clark was asking the referee to leave any additional testimony of his in the closet. But all became parliamentary table matters, when the ruling was set. F. Lee Bailey argued that it was the Head Hunters who had put it out there—the **BELL LETTER**, that is. Clark indicated that that shouldn't make any difference. Ito ruled that his earlier ruling would remain intact.

The jurors came back to Ito Parks and Fields where F. Lee Bailey began his cross. It was smooth, methodical and meticulous. Clark began a rendition of objections. Bailey continued to lay out everything about this witness—from his **GED** to his forty-seven units of college studies, to his tour of duty in the Marine's. Fuhrman was obviously nervous, noticeable by his short breathing exercises between his answers. Fuhrman's smoothness remained visible, but he had this underlying, uneasiness about him. He couldn't quite get enough air into his diaphragm, but was holding his composure nonetheless.

F. Lee Bailey had been limited by referee Ito but bit by bit, Fuhrman let the defense into some pertinent line-of-questioning on background issues. Mark Fuhrman was trying to settle down, but his body language was tellingly on the edge. Bailey had not thrown any cannonballs, as **An Ode to Satire** had promised . . . well, not yet anyway. It was starting to be obvious that Bailey was psychoanalyzing Fuhrman's demeanor. But he wouldn't be broken. After all, he was a Marine. Marines don't break. So the psychology game was underway.

Bailey was beginning to relax this hostile witness, but obviously Fuhrman knew he was simply being set up. He was no fool. Bailey's cadence had begun to flow with a rhythmic harmony . . . well, until Ito asked for a side-bar. This side bar seemed designated to redirect Bailey's modus operandi. He could only throw limited balls with changes in his rhythm. Was he making some headway? Let's wait and see.

Testimony and cross examination was starting to be clear, as to the limitations put on Bailey by Ito. He wasn't doing so well. Ito had boxed him in on his cross. This strategy proved successful to the Head Hunters and was surely noticeable with Fuhrman's professionalism as a witness. He was good, very good in the witness box—very poised within his nervousness.

Many viewers were of the mind that Bailey's episode with Fuhrman would be a 'grandiose,' or 'got-ya' kind of testimony-in-cross. Perhaps an Ali prediction type—like, 'having fun in one,' 'checking out in two,' 'the key in three,' 'more in four,' and, 'flying hi in five.' But, really, most thought a knock-out punch would come early on. It didn't happen. Bailey's world renowned massage type of lawyering was less than emeritus and as of now, hasn't led to a favorable climate—surely not before today's lunch break.

Will Bailey pounce on Mark Fuhrman when their exchange starts up again tomorrow? I don't know. But I've been camping out at Ito Parks and Fields to find out. Seats are limited.

I should let you in on MY secret—I'm ashamed of myself . . . my country . . . the legal system . . . the media. When you put it all together and you take out the population factor, we are left with a trial that is negative, and in many ways is a psychological juggernaut.

(March 14, 1995)

Wrought with the woes of yesteryear's labor, Bailey continued on with his presentation—a **ROGUE COP** was on the loose. He was sure of it. His plan was to niche open a passageway in testimony; a passageway that had been closed by Referee Ito—a passageway to the Truth.

Defense attorneys across this nation were growing excited. Prosecutors were dismayed. All were waiting for the unexpected. Bailey was almost there, but it didn't happen. His opportunity had been negated—manipulated otherwise by Umpire Ito, at side bar.

Here's how it went. The day had started with a discovery hearing which laid favor on the Defense, but F. Lee Bailey had cleverly opened an additional field of inquiry for further testimony.

Fuhrman was looking like a different witness today. One could not readily see this physiological phenomenon, not with the naked eye anyway. This was usually done by focusing on (this calls for a smile) nit-picking things, like mannerism, body-language, etc, and other petty details. Bailey appeared over-vintage and testy. And this notion seemed to be everyone's first high-sign of this matrimonial high light, this nuptial grandstanding—promised early on between these two.

It all started early on when everyone noticed that Fuhrman seemed to be craving more water between fewer questions today. He looked calm, but I don't think that was the case. His answers were nervous ones, but straight-faced. He was in an "I don't know, I don't remember" mode.

The surprise question . . . "Do you intend to gain from this trial," Bailey asked, "through a claim of defamation?" "Yes!" Fuhrman replied. And this answer became a new turn toward new testimony, a new line of thought, and a new ideology. Side bar was then entertained. Will this line of questioning, requested by Bailey, be allowed?

No! . . . Not by this **LEANING TOWER OF PISA**. Once again, ZEUS, the greatest god has diverged to side bar and again will hand-cuff Bailey and the Dream Team Defense Machine. Bailey was entering an area that was going to incriminate Fuhrman's credibility as an officer. Ito seemed determined otherwise; he had been a prosecutor once himself and knew this game very well. A sad day for the Defense I should say. This happened right at the time Fuhrman was becoming most receptive and open and perhaps honest. Ito put a complete stop to this line of questioning, by first diverging to side-bar and then allowing one question, to see where it was going to take this witness. By this time, Fuhrman had evidently recollected his thoughts and once again Bailey was back at square one.

Bailey had needled this witness into new testimony, as lawyers do when they have been hand-cuffed by judges. This witness was on the verge of saying more than he realized would hurt him. In this case, Bailey smelled a rat. However, this rat had a nose of its own, but was opening new inroads to a new roadmap for the Defense's theory that—**THIS WAS A ROGUE COP**. In summary: the niche had been exposed; Bailey had taken a different direction; and Fuhrman was breaking. But, Ito, like Zeus, had restored this testimony back to square one, but later that would not matter.

(March 15, 1995)

With capital productions of over Two Hundred Million Dollars floating through every interested hands, (more than the GNP of the country of Granada) and more revenues anticipated in excess of a Billion Dollars, the question becomes, why? Why are Americans and others across these lands so interested in THIS particular trial? Why not be interested in Susan Smith's (with the two beautiful babies). She pushed her youngsters in a lake. **What about Colin Ferguson's Trial, the Long Island Train slaughterer.** What about the Menendez brothers who killed their parents. What about the trial in Georgia where an ex-husband killed both his spouses and their youngster, or West Palm Beach where Pauline Ziles caused her daughter's death by failing to protect the child from abuse. The state is seeking the death penalty against her. There are many trials similar to these above and perhaps others are even more atrocious (yet all are cruelly streaked with passion and madness). The difference in these trials has been in speculation and appearance. Two words make the difference, **CELEBRATED and RACE.** But that particular note will call for honesty and internalization. Following is . . . .

Ideology that need-be put to rest—I'll try to do that. This is a great time to do our readers a favor and tell them what is possibly going on in this entire trial/fiasco. With the integral media-waves and with all of them seemingly in a frenzy of explanations on the Mark Fuhrman segment of the Orenthal Simpson Series, it's now time to let the cat out of the hatch. Perhaps the honesty of this entire case-in-trail is simply TWO NATIONS—Black and White—divided, and with liberty and justice for each. Sorry, that's the way it appears. Now . . . even that statement needs some refining for clarification. I'll try to do that also.

By all estimation, Minorities have a deep-hearted feeling that American justice has not been fairly played on their playing fields. They have seen the very justice which was written by Anglo Americans played out very differently than its initial intentions and operating in a lopsided mode against them. That very issue militates them to anger. Sadly, or maybe not—but, many Christian Afro Minorities carry some non Christian baggage in their reportage. They are intentionally forcing their issues by being as nonsensical as their foes. They think that if seventy-five percent of Anglo Americans believe this man is guilty before his trial, then, that same percentage on the other side has found a need to intention the same well-deserved mean-spiritedness. It's a way for them to even the playing field without being slaves to a well known history in their past—GUILTY WITHOUT TRIAL. Hangings were a spectacle back then. But of course, well-meaning

Afro-Americans would rather play by the rules which were mostly set by Anglo-Americans. But they are very upset by the mismanagement of fairness of Anglo-American laws whom they think have been punishing the **poor for the sins of the rich**.

Here is what they saw as unfair at the very outset of these games. Polls revealed that approximately seventy-five percent of Anglo-Americans were now exposing what minorities previously had envisioned of them—subtle, but deep-rooted biases in this game-of-sorts. It was now being made known through the media—Court TV. This group, as well as some few Afro-Americans, had declared Orenthal to be guilty—long before the trial. (Both sides were guilty as sin—pro and con.) But, here's the take on the minority group. It was believed that Anglo-Americans, and some few Afro-American females, had finally reached their true impasses, their real feelings about interracial affairs. Many knew that most Americans, overall, were trying very hard to get around this issue, but couldn't, because now, with this particular trial, the issues belied these deep-rooted biases through the trial itself.

One important exception remained . . . the sad emotion one feels for two wonderful human beings, who were brutally killed. They had been the expose' of this deadly disease of racism. This issue was continuing to dilute the greatness of our system. It has, it is, it will, and it shall continue to beat the negative path across America's REAL, TRUE and TRIED DESTINY. And, until Americans reach an honest understanding of themselves and of this issue of racism—that they should be ONE NATION, WITH LIBERTY AND TRUE JUSTICE FOR ALL, most everything will remain the same. Failure will be on the rise. Until this issue is squarely faced and planted properly, honestly and fairly in the virtuous mold of this society—nothing will change anything.

Some Christians have a name for this America—Sodom and Gomorrah. I wouldn't go that far. But, it is at least demonstrative of the American division in their minds. Many minorities think that a great sin of some sort is brewing and brewing and brewing.

For the most part, minorities want to believe in America. They want to believe that most all Anglo Americans are good honest human beings. For most of them, belief and trust is Christian. But, they see a sometimes tricky Anglo-American History, continuing to prevail as status-quo in the crevices of their society. The above is a problem for minorities. They have said that if Orenthal Simpson is guilty, then he should be punished. That doesn't bother them. But, they are saying, don't punish him with an outside decision. Not before one follows the civility of law—in setting the standards for this country and its letter of the law. Anything otherwise, doesn't gel very well with them anymore. That has been their growing problem, and it will continue to be their problem until it is rectified. White supremacy—a fallacy I should say—but is also a problem with them and from a Christian standpoint they can't envision fairness in that ideology, because they know that only God is supreme. They know that color is only skin deep and they understand that. They feel that Anglo and Afro-Americans are on a different page—and with many Anglo-Americans operating with an unfair ideology—but not all.

While Afro-Americans know that a segment of Anglo-Americans are trying to be sincere about being color-blind, minorities yet remain psychologically cornered in their thinking. They also feel a strong ness in saying that no Anglo-American, or Jewish person, has walked a full mile in their shoes. So, many see America as a country, not Americans as individuals. That's sad. And the blame doesn't weigh-in at one corner of this world. Each is to blame—Anglo, and Afro-Americans—both. We are all connected to the Circle of Life, they are saying.

Finally, Minorities have a great spirituality for forgiveness. But they are not willing to be duped again and again—not knowingly—not with their memories and experiences of American slavery. This by-product has been their cautious mainstay. They can't get past this, and they won't without honest change. If this was a card game, a great percentage of its players would quickly say, "I'm ready, but first, IT'S YOUR PLAY." And that's the way it is, and perhaps the way of many of these jurors.

We now go back to the ORENTHAL WORLD SERIES and all of their GAMES.

Today's games started with an array of flashy maneuvers from F. Lee Bailey. It was obvious he was going to pull out his big guns today. He was armed and dressed for war. Fuhrman, a real centurion by nature, was always in a warrior's mode. Will this war between the two be won by brawn or brains—a handsome centurion, or a wise old man? Kudos properly awaits the victor.

Bailey's strategic exercises don't seem to stimulate Fuhrman. He just doesn't seem to be affected unfavorably by any of his theatrics.

The honesty of this witness is becoming a problem for Bailey. The defense is promising support from certain witnesses, but it's not happening. It is beginning to look very bad on the Defense's team and their credibility. The Dream Team will have to do some considerable dreaming to overcome their bruises. **Fuhrman has been an ACHILLES HEEL for them.**

Oops . . . F. Lee Bailey has just blown-up—an explosion of such magnitude as to get him what he wants. (Temper tantrums work with babes, why not with the grown?)

Ballistic, that's where Bailey went today; he went ballistic. Ito would hardly allow him any latitude of entry to the time-of-day, or anything else on new testimony. Ito wants to get these games moving along. I think he's running just a little late now. So, while Marcia Clark was suggesting financial sanctions and other things unfavorable on Bailey's persona, that's when he lost it. He sprang from his seat, pushed along side Clark at the podium, then screamed at the judge. Bailey was trying to force the great Zeus to cause Marcia Clark to give him more respect. After all, he was F. Lee Bailey, Apollo, god of the sun. In game terms, he was the BABE RUTH of his time. He was losing his high batting average, so he wanted to force the umpire of these games to cause young Pandora (Marcia Clark) to respect his position. Head Hunter Clark turned her back to the older gent, coveted the area and with a female attitude (whatever that is), directed Bailey to sit down and shut up, "I have the podium." She had already called him a liar just before, which was the main reason he had jumped from his seat anyway. Now she was shunning his opportunity to conserve his respect. Ito asked Bailey to control himself. "Miss Clark has the floor," he said. Well, he did control his outward emotions, but he didn't exactly calm down. He remained upset. This lawyer was really fighting for his client,—despite having been hand-cuffed by the great Zeus (a metaphor for now). Bailey, also, is later hand-cuffed for a personal problem.

(March 16, 1995)

Ito started this session asking each side to accept the other's forgiveness and apologies for their negative remarks and exchanges yesterday. They did, but Zeus—well!

Fuhrman is back at the plate being thrown many of the same (balls) questions by Bailey. This question came up also—N.V.N. **Nora, Victor,** Nora was some kind of a Marine thing between them. They both had been Marines. **MARINE TO MARINE, N.V.N.,** (Nora, Victor, Nora a two-way radio code never explained) was the question Bailey would leave in the minds of many—the jurors and others. Bailey put the question to Fuhrman and the viewers, "had this ever been used on his two way radio." Fuhrman said, "No." Bailey said, "No more questions."

We will get back to this Fuhrman issue later on. Here's why. I really think Fuhrman will be in trouble with this lawyer and this situation. Fuhrman is believed to have engaged in a testo-lie (making up a lie for testimony). He said he had never used the 'N' **WORD**, ever and never. That, anyone who said he had, was a liar. I think that includes his psychiatrist also. This Doctor has written evidential testimony that will impeach Fuhrman's current testimony, "**never and ever.**"

Officers Frank Sprangler, an LAPD, is now on the stand. He is verifying Mark Fuhrman's whereabouts during the investigation.

Darryl Smith, a free lance photographer, working for Inside Edition on this case, took most of the moving pictures at the Bundy crime scene. He would verify the video.

Det. Phillip L. Vannatter, Det. Tom Lange's partner, a detective since 1971 in robbery homicide, methodically followed the crime scene as Head Hunter Chris Darden lay out and directed him to. A normal morning if I might say so—and well deserved.

Lunch Break

After lunch-break, Darden, the THANATOS of mythology—the Child of Night in the Myth—really was doing a good at the civilized pitching and catching game with Vannatter. This pitch and catch action was the best example yet of baseball being on strike. In other words, nothing was happening, nothing was going on—just pitch and catch, pitch and catch. Rookies they seem to be . . . . No! I'm not for seeing a rookie game, so think I'm going to sleep. Wake me when it's over . . . Perhaps Thanatos too . . . It should be morning by then. If it wasn't for those ants in Darden's pants and him wanting to dance, I really think the Child of Night would put me to sleep. But, hooray!! For Pandora!—She's waiting in her dugout.

There haven't been any objections lately with this new witness; so possibly, F. Lee Bailey is on deck once again for the next cross examination with Det. Vannatter. We will see.

Clarence G. Hanley

(March 17, 1995)

The games will start later than expected today. Ito Parks and Fields had a bomb threat. Of course, writers, media and spectators, when short of explosives of some kind, or show-an-tell of another, or courtroom action, will welcome bomb threats, even actual explosions, wars, fights, any excitement, etc. It's vintage barbarism for most. It's a mainstay for some and till yet for others, their breath of life, their hunger, their thirst for theater, and cinema. Yesteryear's arenas, they would thirst to see blood—like in the Roman Empire. Quite honestly, today's thirst portrays little difference. Worst of all, each of us are saying 'look yonder'—that's the way we do it to keep from internalizing our personal behaviors. But when I point at someone else, I always notice—three fingers are pointing back at me.

After an hour or so Vannatter was back at the plate, he was batting with a few fouls against him (testo-lies). Darden was back also, but should have perhaps gone to the latrine before returning. He appeared needing to have gone to the **LITTLE BOYS ROOM**. He continued to have those 'ants in his pant.' I'm not sure of the name of the dance he was doing—it wasn't the WATUSI. But his body language seemed to be the funniest thought for perhaps a dance I could conjure-up, today. He's kind of funny—well funny enough for satire . . . I'm sure he's very smart, also. But, his body language makes for good satire.

Some issues were centered on, when Orenthal returned from Chicago. He was not a suspect—they were saying—but they had put handcuffs on him. Vannatter said that he did not put them on him, that, in his mind, he was not their final suspect at that time. He didn't take them off of him either; that was a part of the problem. This hand-cuff testimony is going to be a problem for Prosecution in cross examination. They had handcuffed this man before reading him his rights and against his will. Notably, he was willing to be there. He came back from Chicago, just to be an intricate player in the play-offs of this series. He's now under player contract, perhaps for life. Who knows?

NINTH WEEK

(March 20, 1995)

Shapiro goes up against Vannatter, not Bailey. During his cross, he presents Orenthal's hands to the jurors (and fingers too), up close. Darden objected, but to no avail.

Not much ROCK THROWING, HAND-CUFFING, NAME CALLING, or THEATRICS at Ito Parks today. Not much to do for people like myself. If I was there, perhaps I could hang out at concessions, or something. Anyway I could hardly play the video version of the well known game of MONOPOLY either. I needed another player.

Oh yes! There was this dry overcast. Today, I noticed, it was psychological, I suppose, but I hadn't seen signs of any rain, dew, or any great Zeus forecast either. Nothing happening hardly, but, that's okay, some good hitters are coming to the deck soon, I can wait. Meanwhile . . . .

Everyone has been wondering if Orenthal was making any significant headway with his money, toward exoneration. In other words—in the thinking of the **MONOPOLY GAME** itself—was **he PASSING GO?** . . . Was he getting any proof-positive opportunities from CHANCE? . . . Was he going to be able to buy any more HOUSES on PARK AVENUE, or was it Rockingham, or Greta Green? No one is sure about FINES, as everyone well knows. But for sure, we've been watching Orenthal NOT PASS GO, but instead, he did **GO STRAIGHT TO JAIL.** And yes, my gut feelings tell me, Monopoly has to be a lot like capitalism, get what you can, while you can. There are no promises. Lately, there haven't been any promises for ORENTHAL, or his DREAM TEAM DEFENSE MACHINE.

NEWS FLASH on the Eastern side of Courts, Colin Ferguson, continues to out-wit that system, well for another day at least. There was to be a possible verdict today, but Colin Ferguson forced forbearance and in my estimation, a less than worse sentencing, or perhaps an appeal down the road. We will keep you posted.

(March 21, 1995)

Yesterday, when Shapiro had taken Vannatter from the initial crime scene, at Bundy, to Orenthal's home at Rockingham, clearly, Vannatter had demonstrated a different reason for making this trip. Shapiro was doing an excellent job impeaching Vannatter's earlier direct, by Christopher Darden. Something was not adding up in the minds of the Defense. Vannatter and his investigation team had really been sloppy, but there was something more and they were seeking to find out what it was.

Remembering, we are not even half way through these games yet, and only the Prosecution has brought it's hitters to the batter's box. More is yet to be seen.

It appears that Illegal Search and Seizure Laws (the Fourth Amendment), remain an issue. Police conduct and a rush to judgment had not left the Defense's agenda either—even as Shapiro seemed to be distancing himself from the rest of the team.

Today, Shapiro stayed the course.

But in all honesty, I really don't think the Defense can make much gain for their team, not in their current posture. You see, each player seems to be playing a different game. The question should be asked of each player in an effort to get organized, "Who wants to play baseball?" or, otherwise, "Who wants to play monopoly" because, some of their players are giving the appearance of playing different games. They are veering off on their own, and in other directions. That will not help their client. Don't they call that malpractice?—Or something. Maybe Shapiro's pin-wearing, and some other oddities on the defense side, are psychological maneuvers.

A rush to judgment was an obvious choice made by the LAPD. I don't think they can get around that. That was also the game the Dream Team was playing against them. Really, this item becomes an on-the-fence issue. Policemen have to be in that mode of thinking. Their problem in this game is that they are all lying about it. They didn't need to do that. Most of us have done that, we have **RUSHED TO A DECISION** about this case. Anyway, the opinion polls are showing that. So, Shapiro was in good form in gaining some ground in his effort.

Brian 'KATO' KAELIN, now a movie actor/radio announcer who's getting work (never had much before), is now in the catcher's box. Clark is throwing him some practice balls. Everyone else is watching to see how well he's going to catch from her. I thought he had aspired from an acting part in APOTHECARY. However, they say, he doesn't do that sort of acting, or do they say different? Anyway, he was a close friend of Nicole's. But he was residing at the Rockingham address with Orenthal—FREE and GRATIS, it was.

(March 22, 1995)

WHAT NEXT HOLLYWOOD, because everyone knows—the show must go on.

'KATO' KAELIN meets the bill in keeping the Orenthal show on the road. Laughter and pleasantries were in order. This day belonged to him. I'm not sure yet whose team he's on, but pitch and catch continues with him and Head Hunter Clark. He's got her on a SAFARI and he's the head honcho. This expedition is not settling very well with her, not under afore circumstances. We'll know more when the Dream Team cross examines.

(March 23, 1995)

BOY IMPISH ('KATO'), (PHENIUS, a bard in the palace), was known by many names in his ploy to gain an advantage in personal opportunities. Where this ruse will take him, no one really knows. Capitalism has a way of producing negative character-ism. Subtle cases are no different.

OPPORTUNITY and MOTIVATION were the avenues Clark was pursuing. She had gotten opportunity out of Boy Impish, but was having a hard time obtaining motivation. He was holding on and not offering all damaging testimony that Orenthal was sometimes of a mean-spirited nature.

It was starting to be impossible for PHENIUS to be a great player for the Head Hunters if he couldn't help show **MOTIVATION**. Kato had not been moved in that direction as a player for the Prosecution. He was somewhat reluctant and was being a wild card player. In fact, he was acting out similarly for both teams. He remained in that posture under cross examination—straddling the fence as it were. But, under direct, Clark had grilled him to no end.

Shapiro, of the Dream Team, operating without a Kato contract (Kato was not his witness) succeeded as a side-liner and a deal maker. He cross-examined the supposing Head Hunter player, Kato, and with little effort made him a defensive player-player. For Clark, **PHENIUS** had veered the fence—and to such an extent that it seemed better for her to impeach his testimony. She had gotten most of what she wanted, but impeaching this witness will come back to haunt the Head Hunters. Mark my words.

Here's what's happening. Since **Brian 'KATO' (PHENIUS) Kaelin's** attendance at Ito Parks and Fields, I've seen bunt after bunt and hardly, if any, run from either team. There have been some few laughs, a degree of grilling, some icing on the cake and a little smooth talking by Shapiro. Today's game had a mild, somewhat negative overcast, hovering over the Prosecutors camp and dugout. While neither team has really scored big, the Head Hunters have surely been set back by player crossover. Kato had played both ends against the middle for his own advancement, which will surely harm him in the long run.

The Dream Team has likewise gathered a disjointed overcast—by veering in different player directions. Bad move—Shapiro exposed to the media, on his own, his deepest, cornered wish **(not to play the RACE CARD)**. At that moment, his statement surely did not look like team effort, team support, or even team positioning. Shapiro, sometimes called ATLAS, carrier of the sky (MYTH), was SETTING OUT alone in LAPD HAVENS. He was displaying a tag in support of the LAPD. Their players were now starting to look like a dream and not much like a Team. We will let this jury type, run amok activity, play itself out and keep you posted. The pundits will do that for me.

Clarence G. Hanley

TENTH WEEK

(March 27, 1995)

Considering that Shapiro was mistakenly asking several question of Kato and referring to the wrong Orenthal finger, I question a lawyers net worth in making such a mistake. At Four to Six Hundred Dollars an hour, a lawyer has to operate near perfection in such a case as this. Personally, I would get no justice at all—guilty or not guilty, having watched this game of lawyering. It's pay as you go. The Dream Team has made many mistakes—some of which are inexcusable.

Kato had been rather humorous last week, but not so today. Clark made him a serious witness, very serious. Now, he was to be strung up and hung out to dry. Ito was asked to make him a hostile witness for her side.

Prosecution's redirect was starting to be overkill with questions to Kato-the-time-bomb. It is intuitive thinking, but surely the juror's plates were filled with this testimony and too many days for too few items. Some of these issues had to be dead dogs with jurors and were surely nearing a matter of "I don't care" information, ("Been there. Heard that.") Some jurors have to finally be saying, "So what!" if

Orenthal had indicated to Kato that, me and Nicole are finished, so what, If he alluded to it twice or three times before. So what! If he appeared upset with some human emotions; we all have those. So what! If he questioned his former wife wearing of mini skirts, as a bad influence for his children. So what! if he had a girl friend nearing their final spousal episodes as divorcees." Here's the central question, did he or did he not kill his ex-wife and Ron Goldman? Because really, the search for the truth has foul-balled itself way, way, out into the left field grandstands. At this rate none of us—with all of our abilities—will achieve respectable retrieval of the status quo as a great civic society. The world is watching. They want to know if AMERICAN JURISPRUDENCE, operating as a Democracy, really works. It's time for show and tell.

In a little while Ito would ask, "Haven't we gone over this before?" Clark was hammering away at lead questions now, bit by bit. She could do that—she had declared Kato a hostile witness.

Shapiro had done his job when he got Kato to show that most of Prosecution's redirects with him, were mostly matter-of-fact testimonies. That Orenthal was having natural human emotions, no different from others, and that he was not being of hostile character.

When Shapiro asked Kato if he was intimidated by Marcia Clark and her position, and he answered in the affirmative this was a turning-of-the-tide for everyone's thinking. The question starts to ring loud and clear—a 'why not' question. That is . . . the police/prosecution side of many such issues can be scary for many citizens of our society, especially, those who have not seen that part of their government being their friend. Others may see it differently.

Kato seemed so sincere when asked by Shapiro, "Had he done everything he could to be honest and truthful with these jurors." He replied, "Yes! I'm trying, but my memory is sometimes a problem." One surely becomes a Kato fan club member when he, with boyish sincerity and appropriate of body language, asserts, "Your Honor, I'm trying to be as honest and as truthful to the best of my recollection, sir."

The word UPSET had a totally different inference, when Shapiro's style of questioning was put to Kato. Unlike the prosecution with him, Shapiro's questions were non-confrontational. As commentator/pundits connoted, questioning in the Shapiro manner perhaps supported this witness against his most noted fears and feelings. He had not been comfortable at all with Prosecution, even as he afforded truthful efforts. He was trying to remember.

Projected results of this witness remains to be seen.

(March 28, 1995)

I suspect Prosecution's last several witnesses (Fuhrman, Vannatter, and Kato) have been detrimental to the dreams of the Dream Team's Defense Machine. Will Orenthal be packing his bags for a long one way trip? Feelings are going back and forth each week. Today, it seems so. But there is yet a long way to go.

When Clark had finished beating the last witnesses to death, she then came back and beat them some more, including Kato. Whoever said, "You cannot get blood from a turnip" had not met Head Hunter Clark. This lady is not taking any prisoners. She just doesn't have the time nor the space, evidently. Clark, clearly, has one thought in mind: Go for the jugular—and win. This man had been every woman's problem. To her, Orenthal was the root (perhaps her ex-husband had been one of the stems) and it was time to cut the root. It was time to hold it high in the air for all to see and like THE vigorous leader of the AMAZONS, proclaim victory to the world.

A new day had dawned. Men should no longer be the nightmare to diligent, assiduous shoppers and buyers of an array of goods and services. They would now be the PRODUCERS of goods and with little or no control. In other words, once men have properly been put in their places, women could properly take their rightful place in society—as Mall Queen Shoppers.

Rachel Ferrara, a friend of Kato Kaelin's, did her bit to support her man friend.

Then came Allan Park, he was the Limo driver. He seemed honest, but questionable. He is a wearer of glasses and now being asked to tell everything he saw the night in question. But, he wasn't wearing his glasses that particular night. In some people's estimation, his lack of clear vision has no place here, where absolute testimony is necessary. But he continued to link the time line for the Prosecution. He was batting better than average in doing SO.

(Something to watch out for) Allan Park made entry to Orenthal's home that same night. He had no memory of seeing blood spots, was his testimony. But he wasn't wearing his glasses either. He, however, saw a silhouette, contoured in the dark of the night, formed in the size of a black man—six feet and two hundred pounds. Big deal! It was O. J. He lived there you know. The man was a promenade of his grounds and estate—not an odd habit for some.

The most to be said at this moment is, to repeat, this game still has a long way to go.

(March 29, 1995)

ALLAN PARK parked himself back under oath and again was being crossed examined by Johnnie Cochran. He said under oath that he saw two cars parked in Orenthal's driveway. Other testimony will say that was not so, not at the time he says he saw the two cars in Orenthal's driveway. Orenthal's daughter, Arnelle, contended that her car would not have been parked there until later, after her dad had left for the airport. This is a crack in Prosecution's testimony, and with a very good witness. The Defense will say, well . . . Allan, just maybe you didn't see all you said you thought you saw.

Each witness gets the chance to see a live poker game being played between each side in this series. Here is what will happen. The team that plays their hand the best—wins the game. That's all there is to it. But with one difference; a referee can cause a shift in each play of the game.

Judge Delbert Wong, a Special Master for Orenthal's travel bags, was now on the stand. Everything was logical and there were no explosions.

James William was the Skycap who had checked Orenthal's bags June 12, 1994. They were just regular bags to him. Williams had not analyzed the two bags he saw, or the one Orenthal was carrying. As a tip, he received a Twenty Dollar Bill, but gave Orenthal Ten Dollars Change. Those numbers will be very important on both sides as the case progresses along.

(March 30, 1995)

Susan Silva took the stand today. Nothing significant to our purposes occurred. However, she did clarify the security equipment at the Orenthal Estate.

Shaun Chapman, a past Public Defendant (now on the Defense's team, and was happy to be there) had her first day on the playing field at Ito Parks and Field. She crosses examined Susan Silva for a few short minutes. Everyone seemed happy that she could pitch and was glad she had gotten some Showtime.

Some additional DNA Discovery was held today. Most notable—he looked like a newcomer but he wasn't—was Professor William Thompson. He spoke eloquently and with great wisdom about DNA subject matter. He was speaking about PRELIMINARY FACTS BEFORE THE JUDGEMENT VERSUS FACTS AND ISSUES IN FRONT OF A JURY. We will explain this game at a later date. You will be hearing more about this subject as both sides argue rights Orenthal gave up back in January of 1995—perhaps a defensive strategy.

(March 31, 1995)

Cameramen and their supervisor, for the city of L.A., came to testify on television—their moment in pictures and TV. They will testify about having also been a part of this world-renowned spectacle. As I said before, everyone has been vying for a position for their MOMENT IN THE SUN. Each also knew that if they could just add the slightest TWIST in their SOUND BITES, CHURN the pneumatical thinking one DEGREE pro POPULACE, STICK their NOSES in front of ANY camera lens that was plugged into this JURISPRUDENCE HISTORY FALLACY, or wave a BANDWAGON FLAG in pursuit of PROSECUTION OBJECTIVITY, their possibilities of going down in JUSTICE HISTORY would be greatly enhanced.

Charles Cale, a witness who claims to have seen the Bronco at a strategic time, came out of the woodwork for his moment in the sun. He also could be detrimental to the Defense.

ELEVENTH WEEK

(A DNA PREVIEW AND ITS COLLECTION)

This story play-by-play commentary is now moving into another area of arguments—**COLLECTION OF EVIDENCE for DNA**. We must keep in mind that our democratic jurisprudence System is designed and bound in proving ones innocence against ones guilt and BEYOND A REASONABLE DOUBT. This is standard proof in all criminal cases.

DNA, in the Simpson case, is being used as proof of guilt beyond a reasonable doubt. It is not proof of absolute certainty however, only mathematical probability. It is not a verdict of proof beyond a shadow of a doubt, or even proof of scientific certainty. It is, however, the highest standard of PROOF known to the LAW. There is no higher standard. That is what the jurors will be focused on—that standard. The burden of proof will be put upon the government and the L.A. Prosecution.

"It is not possible that someone could be convicted on DNA alone," says Judge Gerald Sheindlin, acting Supreme Court Justice in the Bronx of New York. He objectifies that you will not have five hundred, a thousand, or three hundred thousand suspects that are involved in the case. There are only a few people usually involved. It's very easy if you have one in one hundred thousand probabilities when you pull the fish from the dragnet. If you have only two or three people, one is most probably the culprit and the other two will probably be eliminated.

So, here are the issues and questions involved. ARE YOU DOING THE TESTING CORRECTLY? Two, HOW DO YOU INTERPRET THE RESULTS? Another question will be, IS DNA TESTING AS FOOL-PROOF AS FINGER PRINTING? IS IT INDEED GENETIC FINGER PRINTING? On both these questions the jury still has need of appraisal.

The last bit of note-telling, on this, is that the Defense will be fighting the mere IMAGE of DNA, which is a science of probabilities. We were all brought up on science, but do we understand its multitudinous substructures? This will also be the big QUESTION MARK.

The world of SPORTS has varied divisions, varied ideals, varied logics and varied enjoyments for different people. The world of SEROLOGY, the study of serum (and in this case DNA), will likely be no different than the area of sports.

Here are some things we know now, for sure. DNA carries a person's hereditary information. For now, we will not say it is exactly like fingerprinting—science doesn't really know yet. But, before this trial, or this game is over, we might have learned some new science. Now, more than ninety-nine percent of all DNA is the same for everyone—is the on-going school of thought. There are areas between the genes called polymorphic regions. These areas vary dramatically between individuals. These are the areas that are tested.

There are two basic types of DNA test. One is PCR for Polymerase Chain Reaction. This is a copying process wherein a small piece is copied up to millions of times. It provides less information than another we will introduce, RFLP. PCR takes less than two weeks to test.

The second type is RFLP, lettered for Restriction Fragment Length Polymorphism. This takes up to twelve weeks to test and requires a larger sample. However, it is much more definitive. But it is fair to ask, if it is fully fair to the defendant. Because, and here's the rub, it is not one hundred percent definitive.

Now, here is what you should know. Our criminal justice system is not based on one hundred percent certainty. Keep that in mind—that's very, very important. We are a civilization of laws; that's our survival system. Keep that in mind also. Without our system of laws, we would be glorified barbarians. That could be a consideration for any individual—his personal choice, so to speak. But, in our country, we are expected to follow the letter of the law—even though they can be questionable at times.

NOW BACK TO SATIRE

(April 3, 1995)

I think last week marked the end of search for MOTIVE. Prosecution would have wanted to be much further ahead than they are. As they moved into COLLECTION OF EVIDENCE, they were expected to lose some ground. The BLOOD TRAIL they were on, however, should get lots of attention and should be very much in their favor. I think a twist will be forthcoming.

If it were not for the science of FORENSICS and DNA, all else would have just become many little battles of rhetorical wars. But now, the WAR will be on DNA. Then ultimately, the decision—predicated on the science itself, and interjected with or without reasonable doubt.

Many avid viewers, who have decided against the accused, will not like the **REASONABLE DOUBT** part of their vaunted jurisprudence—perhaps not until the tables are turned against them. Many are guaranteed that sooner are later by the law of averages, the tables will be turned. In other words, we should accept the fact that human nature is expected to follow the law of diminish and return.

Many things in life have a way of coming back to where they started.

Today, Det. Bert Luper, a Simpson Case investigator along with Det. James Harper, continued to answer questions about photography. Bits and pieces were being carved out of each officer by the Defense. The Prosecutors stayed their course with these officers also—in an effort to prove their theory. (One officer will later become their worse nightmare.)

The hearing from the Defense's viewpoint, however, is continuing to show the public how sloppy the LAPD had been.

Topping off all else, another video has surfaced—this time by the fault of the Prosecution. They had not informed the Defense, on this, at any time in discovery, and now their hands are going to be slapped.

Marcia Clark was asked to give an opening statement about this mystery tape, by Umpire Ito—not under oath though. (Oh, the games people have played in this series!) Well, we can expect the Prosecution to be sanctioned for this boo-boo. If for nothing else, just to even the playing field a bit. This umpire loves this misnomer, of psychic—in producing an even playing field. Who does he favor? Many will ask. I don't know, many will say. But he surely favors an even playing field—at the start of each game. I really think, as a judge, he would like to see where the real truth lies and with distinct clarity—so that there will be no doubt in anyone's mind. I don't think that will happen in this case but, if this is his vision, it will be a way of ending the case with his credibility intact.

Criminal-list Dennis Fung's statement back in June of 1994 was that no analysis tests were done at the Bundy scene when collected. Some issues are being raised by Peter Neufeld concerning this topic. It seems now that the defense is going to fight Prosecution on every nit-picking issue of DNA. Prosecutor Deputy District Attorney Hank Goldberg's position is that the tests can be done in a variety of ways.

Both sides will be arguing blood DNA. With blood being found under the fingernails of Nicole, the Defense thinks they have a viable argument. The Prosecution has this big long blood trail that will be the biggest game in town. That trail has been heavily questioned by the Defense, who is also arguing inconclusive evidence on the part of Prosecution. I think that will be left to scientific evidence and the experts.

Dennis Fung, as you know, is the lead Criminal-list in this case. He has been a Criminal-list since 1984 and has lots of education under his belt. But he and his team have really done a messy job (in this case) and it probably is not entirely their fault. LAPD might have a larger fault in this set of misplays. But, the real issues of changing rubber gloves, wiping the sweat off of brows, covering the bodies with used bedding and similar activities, will not help in their search for truth—not through science anyway. This contamination has been an embarrassment for Prosecution.

The Defense is focusing on COLLECTION, QUANTITY and QUALITY with Fung. Fung isn't doing so well in his testimony with cross examiner Barry Scheck. He will soon be impeached through test-o-lying, causing resurfacing of Vannatter, who is expected to be asked back to the plate to batter r r-up again. Its baseball season re-enacting, but this time, Vannatter will be catching without a glove. Fung, in some ways, has taken his glove and perhaps his mask also. In other words, the Prosecution cannot have it two ways—the truth cannot be with both characters in this play.

"WE OUGHT TO GO OUT AND KILL NINE OR TEN OF THOSE ATTORNEYS." These were the words spoken by Doctor Irwin Golden, Forensics and Criminal-list expert for the Prosecution. He was waving a toy gun when he made this statement, and surely no—no by any professional standard. That statement (probably playful), is now coming back to haunt him and the prosecution side. He made these statement months ago after preliminary hearings in which he didn't do well as a witness. The Dream Team took this statement as a personal focus, from him. After all, no other attorneys seemed personally involved in Golden's life at that time they were thinking. Discussions are now going on about this issue.

BLOOD, BLOOD, BLOOD and perhaps more BLOOD; GAMES; GAMES and more GAMES; INNUENDOS, and more INNUENDO; Where does it all stop; No one really knows.

Brian Kelberg sparred with Gerald Uelmen in a war on rulings. Ito became tight-jawed and a bit upset, while Uelmen was speculating and indicting different issues. Ito bluntly asked him to make his point. Ito seemed drained and ready to give up the practices of lawyering and judging. Stress was taking its toll. He was edgy.

Later, when Ito tried to make a joke with Uelmen while he was continuing to make his presentation and discussion on a discovery matter, Uelmen evened the score. Ito tried to make his joke with Uelman by digressing during Uelman's discussion. With this fair game opportunity, Uelman was able to set Ito straight, saying to him, "This is NOT a JOKING MATTER and too often JOKES are out of place." Wooooow . . . and done in the Uelmen manner and style. Ito had no place to go with this response. It was passively accepted by Ito, but . . . ? What a country we live in. In many ancient and sometimes modern societies, Uelman could have been sent to the gallows for such a statement (not necessarily a reckless one, but that's the way it was).

My, my—the heat is here and summertime is a comin' on. BASEBALL IS BACK. L-e-t-s p-l-a-y ball.

(April 4, 1995)

Hank Goldberg of the Prosecution was ready to play. He was batting in the EVIDENCE COLLECTIONS position and seemed over meticulous today with Criminal-list Dennis Fung. He had graphs, drawings, displays, exhibits and charts galore. It was a seminar made for television and prosecutors, of course. But TV pundits weren't impressed, because their rhetoric was centered on, "this could be too much for jurors. What this meticulous display could mean to jurors was wrong doings and malfeasance and the trial itself could become secondary." Well, Prosecution can't win for losing with this pundit bunch.

Special Note, prosecutors were sanctioned for not turning over the latest mystery video tape.

New testimony surfaced with two defense witnesses who are prosecutors. They were the prosecutors in the Rodney King case. They will testify on behalf of the Defense. Their names are Allen Yocosume and Terry White. That should prove to be a time in infamy for the Prosecution. These two will testify to a mock prosecution before facing the batter's box, and it doesn't look favorable to the Head Hunter's side.

He was sanctioned once again and with little or no sincere apology from Hank Goldberg. This will not help the Head Hunter's team. The Prosecution exhibited and made references to an airline ticket. Hank Goldberg was instructed not to do this—twice. He did, and like Darden before, was having a hard time accepting his personal wrong-doing in front of this playing court and Umpire Ito.

Barry Scheck sparked more negative rays of light on Criminal-list Dennis Fung. He has now focused this light on him and, as of this moment, Fung's testimony is not looking very good for Prosecution. A testo-lie seems inevitable. Andrea Mazola, the assistant Criminal-list, had done a bumbling collection job, along with her supervisor and Fung. Now, Fung is almost for sure being impeached—but only because of earlier testimony.

Yesterday, Orenthal was looking very much on the guilty side to many who wanted to lose hope. But today Barry Scheck has displayed a different tune and a different ball game for many. This game and its competition, was back in full bloom. You could hear the crowds jeering as Scheck made some headway for the Dream Team Defense Machine. That didn't faze him; he was swayed by none. Instead, Scheck plowed onward, bound in his cross with Dennis Fung. By the time he finished raising lots of dirty topsoil, and adding some slop (sometimes called fertilizer), corruption seemed visible, inevitable and growing.

Clarence G. Hanley

(April 5, 1995)

Much was the same with Dennis Fung today as he recounted his expose, which included numerous problems with the LAPD Criminal-list's investigation and collection. A testo-lie really did seem forthcoming.

(April 6, 1995)

Two jurors are sick today and there has been another bomb threat. All is well with the bomb threat, but there will be no court activities today.

Since there are no witnesses today, I hope to whet the appetites of many with a pun-of-sorts—my side show. As you might know, dreaming is probably not unlike the toying of these games. Because, this trial has been really puzzling to me and I think everyone else at times and . . . I . . . I . . . I really, really thought . . . .

. . . Well . . . I thought I could hear the sounds of **HARRY CAREY** (the famed baseball sportscaster) prodding himself back into baseball history and this was a sore spot for me. This was my gig now and I didn't need HIS competition. I was the announcer of this Orenthal game-of-sorts. When I sensed his visit approaching, the very thought of his greatness put a crutch in my style. I began to wonder . . . did I need his aid or any additional support, or a prop to pull this SATIRE business off. Couldn't I go on calling and announcing this game the way I saw each play? Was this idea out-of-sorts for me or anyone else for that matter? Had I internalized properly and fairly about this case, this game-of-sorts? Had I been fair in my writings and news casting? Did I take into full consideration, baseball, the game itself—versus an atrocious homicide—and baseball (our favorite pastime) and the system? What about the relatives of the Brown family, or the Goldman family, or the Simpson family? all to be considered—and I did? I thought my aim had been at the jurisprudence system only—with a few add-INS of course. Noted, this homicide, with me, was by happenstance and was only a by-product to make my point of interest. I was using it in a satiric mode to convey some realistic points that Americans were acting distal to. OUR COUNTRY HAD SOME PROBLEMS and we weren't dealing with them very well. The distal sorts, well . . . they didn't think there were any problems at all. They have been asleep. But, deep down within each of them, even they must surely have known our troubled waters.

Well . . . I should not have been upset when I finally realized **HARRY CAREY** had made his occurrence to bequeath me with his proud holdings—his blessings—if I may say a presentation of his holdings of having been the most world-renowned baseball announcer of his time. He had been called the greatest ever and was now visiting 'me.' What an honor!

When I had finally discharged myself from **SOMNOLENCE**, (that is . . . this dreamlike state of fantasy that I was in) and back to a bit of consciousness as I was slipping in and out, I immediately pinched myself. I seemed to be going a little over the cliff, perhaps off my rocker, with this O.J. thing. [I was having a bit of fun doing it, I really should say.] I was awakened by a (Hari-Kari) **HARRY CAREY**, (remembering that phrase and Carey the famed baseball announcer had many). All of this had just been a part of a dream—all of this. But, there is **NO REST FOR THE WEARY**, this game MUST go on and it will—with, or without me. Its come too far and now has no stopping point. Pundits have made it that way—all of them.

In fact, it behooves me to think that I really had been synergistically pinched, perhaps designed to focused me back into reality. My head is once again on straight, or is it.

Awake now and remembering those games in my youthful past and whenever **HARRY CAREY** was announcing (I liked him on radio, you should know). I could always hear a slightly airiest or windiest sound in the background or behind the announcing of the game, there in the windy city of Chicago. He would tell us how beautiful the day was, especially the weather overcastting his baseball park. You could always hear the background noises of the thousands of fans—seemingly designed to fit into the full scheme and theme of things. For me, a lover of baseball, this was a recall of the heart, notched forever in time and my memory. I really am not as good as Harry Carey, but I am announcing this trial-of-a-game the way it feels to me. It feels like satire. It feels like crazy. **It is fanatically crazy.**

(April 7, 1995)

Because of the sick Jurors, (sick is not a metaphor) there will be no courtroom action today at Ito Parks and Fields.

Trying out for first base, Senator Alfonse D'Amato got caught up in the Simpson Series action through a bit of mean-spiritedness of his own. He infuriated the Asian community by making mockery of their society. He was joking on the **Imus Radio Show.** As usual, he apologized—in fact, several times. But, like he says, he knows better and this is not the first time he's made such a foolish blunder. Currently, Ito has not responded to any of his TV apologies. In thinking of one of Ito's favorite clichés—**THE PROBLEM IS** . . . this Senator makes a habit of negativism. He's very mad at something (the budget perhaps) I'm not really sure what, but it seems like he's mad at the world.

TWELFTH WEEK

(April 10, 1995)

No court today.

(April 11, 1995)

Today, for Barry Scheck, there was more than one way to skin a cat, and he was using just about every way he knew to penetrate the obvious evasive testimony of Dennis Fung. Cross examining Fung was like following an entry into a maze where this witness had many outlets. However, Scheck of the Dream Team was destined to corner every outlet and window-of-opportunity. He was leaving no avenues un-examined, no trails un-followed and no testimonies un-tested. As testimony reached the end of this maze, the obvious seemed to stand un-denied. The Head Hunters were about to be beheaded—decapitated away from the **BLOOD TRAIL** and the **DNA** and the **EVIDENCE**, sidetracked into the dimness of **REASONABLE DOUBT**.

Regardless of anything else, Dennis Fung had handled evidence **WITHOUT GLOVES**. He denied it, but it was caught on tape. The homicide glove had been moved also—contaminated as it were. It seems Fung has now entered an area of untruthful testimony, and the Head Hunters can't seem to buy a score. Now . . . with each bunt, Scheck seems to be chipping away at any sizable credibility the Head Hunters may have had. If you are looking at the scoreboard right now, don't! This game still has many home runs to be played out—on both sides.

(April 12, 1995)

This game is not all about the defendant, but . . . a question continues to hang in the balance for many, CAN ORENTHAL BEAT THE RAP, SINCE HE COULDN'T BEAT THE RIDE?—that embarrassing ride he took to JAIL; a reminder of his youthful days, a ride that seemed impossible for him to PASS GO—and he didn't. He went straight to JAIL (referencing the Monopoly Game). Everyone thought he had grown past his boyhood ruses, but we shall see. Many think he should be considered innocent until proven guilty. It's the law, they say. Some are saying otherwise.

Today, conflicting points of views from other witnesses have cast wide shadows of darkness. Barry Scheck now has broadened that light on the LAPD and their criminal-LIST. A TESTO-LIE and perhaps a ROGUE COP will surface soon. Dennis Fung, more and more, has shed a vivid light on such possibilities. Even Fung might have been a part of some wrongdoing, this defense seems anxious to say. We are not sure how, but we are headed in that direction. Some of Mark Fuhrman's story has not jived with some of Fung's witnessing, or that of Det. Tom Lange, or Det. Vannatter. A laboratory document page seems to be missing also, designating some people who did business at the testing laboratory.

Fung is looking ruffled by now, but seems to have the strength to do additional damage to his persona. **He-can't-help-himself**

(April 13, 1995)

Again, today, Barry Scheck was performing near miraculously for his team. He brought home some more big scores. Lawyers across the country were revamping their trial-lawyering strategies, all designed to pattern their plays after him.

Sequestration is taking its toll also and could soon become an overriding issue of the entire trial. A member who was dropped from the jury is now gearing up for some nasty rhetoric and Umpire Ito is lending an ear.

Ito specifically asked each side not to discuss matters under testimony with either side during breaks—since yesterday. Fung violated this request this morning and will have another coffin to carry, as the defense continues to bury him in his testimony.

Some lawyering attitudes by Barry Scheck might be considered acrimonious, but some look upon them as humorous. In the sternest manner Barry Scheck, with his baby-faced, boyish way, queried, **"Mr. FUNG, have you made some bad choices in this case?"**

Dennis Fung: (computing each of his responses), "I don't remember. I'm not sure—maybe."

Scheck: **"What about THAT, Mr. FUNG? Did you see THAT, Mr. FUNG?"** after showing and viewing a tape where Dennis Fung saw another problem with mishandling of collection of evidence.)

Fung: (slowly, recalculating the question over in his mind) "To the best of my recollection, I can't be sure."

A flurry of such questions similar to these above, from Barry Scheck and answers from Dennis Fung, are now synonymous to a witness having been **caned**. I say it now, as I've said it before, no witness will leave this case unscathed.

I suppose the most famous accounting (made fun of) in Fung's testimony when Barry Scheck said in his most New York colloquy (dialogue), snapping at Dennis Fung, **"THERE!! THERE, HOW ABOUT THAT "Mr. FUNG . . . how about that?"** Barry

Scheck once again was thought to have impeached Dennis Fung for some earlier testimony. Fung had seemingly lied about handling materials without gloves. He said he never had handled any materials without gloves. He had, and the video film proved the case.

(April 14, 1995)

Done . . . In the style of this referee. In this case, Referee Ito had again been the LEANING TOWER OF PISA. Like a magician, once again, it was a . . . now you see it, now you don't thing. Ito promised to give a sanction today against the Head Hunters, but once again found reasons to delay, mostly caused by the presence of the famed Marcia Clark—all to the Head Hunters advantage. Ito tried to keep her quiet, but she simply fought to edge in a few one liners (attention-getters) to quash the sanction. This gives Goldberg a great opportunity to rehabilitate the crippled Dennis Fung to the jurors without the sanction being made known. The sanction will be presented to the jurors next week. Thanks to Marcia the Great.

I'm sure you and I would welcome the most of any respect this trial-of-a-game has to offer, but sometimes the players are falling a bit short in their courtroom behaviors. The latest problem is now coming from the Defense. Worst of all, it was in the style of Senator Alfonse D'Amato. Johnnie Cochran was poking fun, singing, "We're going to have fun,

fun, FUNG," and Robert Shapiro was passing out fortune cookies at the courthouse. It all seemed to be in bad taste. Their wisdom can be called into question, proving the point that self-censoring has its place.

THIRTEENTH WEEK

(April 17, 1995)

Charisma could hardly be found anywhere in the vicinity of mundane Hank Goldberg. I almost dozed off to sleep again myself until Umpire Ito frightened me conscious. He had sharply directed Barry Scheck back under his control. **His were near fighting words when he rhetorically snapped the fear into Scheck, "Four times I've told you! Now shut up and sit down . . . <u>Now!</u>"** I wasn't sure what to think. Perhaps I should have felt sorry for this small-stature but brilliant man, Barry Scheck. He is making lots of money, becoming world renowned for helping many, so maybe I shouldn't feel sorry for him at all.

Today, Ito and Barry Scheck just didn't seem to be getting along. Ito, perhaps, upset because he was now realizing this game was moving along much too slowly. Also, Scheck was perhaps being too forceful for Ito. Scheck, last week, had been rated as a model for lawyering across the country and had been placed in very high esteem. Maybe Ito didn't like that. I don't know.

A short fused judge, overbearing lawyers, battles for control; all were playing a part on this playing field at Ito Parks. Fung had been a plus for the Dream Team Defense Machine and Barry Scheck was now their star player outside of his normal jurisdiction, I might add. He had been shipped in from New York City and was being billed as a great hitter at the DNA plate. With Ito's wife being a police captain, and the media checking every dotted 'I' and double-checking every crossed 't', brilliant lawyers were acting like children at play, and this whole situation was being played-out like a game. So, Ito had surely grown irritated. To top it all, this particular witness was an Oriental-American, as to Ito. This witness has been the toy of the season for the defensive team and their star player, Barry Scheck.

Scheck's angle toward Dennis Fung had been, "Have you engaged in a cover-up and is that what you're doing now as a witness?" He then asked Fung the meaning and connotation of a cover-up. After the damage had been done, afterwards, every word under this kind of re-cross examination was detrimental to the Prosecution. The mere fact of the meaning of cover-up would now stand for itself. The question had been framed toward Fung because of his vague and unique way of answering the Defense's questions. Many of his answers came back to haunt him. He had been impeached on a great deal of his testimony, so patching him up again was nearly impossible. He had been **Humpty Dumpy**, who had a great fall, and they were not going to be able to put him back together again.

I think what hurt Fung mostly was that he testified he had done most of the collection of evidence and that his assistant (trainee) had done little to none of it. In actuality, it was the other way around. When all had been said and done, collection of evidence had been the biggest cover-up of all. He had lied, perhaps incriminating himself. He certainly had sullied his official position.

(April 18, 1995)

Barry Scheck today, in his re re-cross, didn't award viewers with any new acrimony. It was starting to be sleepy-time in TV land. He was trying now to beat a dead horse—TO DEATH.

Some busy work takes place as Ito receives complaints from both sides. The Defense is arguing unfair treatment by him. The prosecution will file a motion also, aimed at the courtrooms acts and displays toward the Defense.

(April 19, 1995)

No court today. Among other things, there is a deliberation on jury problems—problems that could lead to a mistrial.

(April 20, 1995)

Andrea Mazzola, an LAPD Criminal-list, is now at bat. Hank Goldberg is pitching direct questions to her, as he did with her co-worker Dennis Fung. Her prepped testimony included her accommodations for collections at the Bundy and Rockingham crime scene—her first.

Mazzola appears more affirming and surer of her testimony than Fung's display. This is very helpful to the prosecution and in some ways; it shores up some of Dennis Fung's testimony, at least to a degree. Of course this is only foresight before defensive cross examination.

Pete Neufelt, Scheck's partner and another defensive DNA expert player from the East coast, takes the pitcher's mound. He is following a record-breaking direct by Hank Goldberg, who finished in three-fourths of a testimonial day. Woooh!

Neufelt's delivery had considerable speed. Each question was shotty, very clear and very concise. You had to be on your P's and Q's as a witness, or you could become entangled. You could also appear to be a **LIE-N-KING**, running rampant in this lawyering jungle. You could perhaps, appear to be another cover-up player. His exchange was civil, but like spit-fire, or spit-balls. Neufelt, a Brooklyn native, was very good at shooting his rhetorical weapon.

Clarence G. Hanley

(April 21, 1995)

A protest is being affected by thirteen jurors today. They are protesting the dismissal of three deputy sheriffs and will not sit as jurors. A single juror simply said she couldn't take it any more, she was going back to her flight attendant job. Consequently, there will be no hits, no plays, no jury, no court and no sense of order today. The limelight has taken its toll and otherwise looks—very much—like London Bridges are now falling down at Ito Parks and Fields. Ito has lost all control and will perhaps; now internalize his miss-direction.

Here is some of the story on those jurors. Jeannette Harris, who was not the first juror to sunder from the rest of the group, has perhaps been the best theater yet on the jury. She has been the best indicator that something has gone desperately wrong with this process. There has been a **COMEDY OF ERRORS** brought to light in this game, which has now become, perhaps, a charade. There is no opportunity for a conviction under these circumstances. But I'm sure this game will throttle along without honest force of steam. The effort will be made, but the damage has been done, and there can be no restoration in this particular show—none. Further, a criminal trial especially this criminal trial is not a search for the truth. **It is a search for the truth THAT IS ADMISSIBLE. There is a difference.**

FOURTEENTH WEEK

(April 25, 1995)

A different playing field was clearly unveiled today and you could tell so. The entire park and field had been refurbished in less than a weekend. Last weekend and before, had been near mayhem for the Empire of Lance Ito. It all had finally come full circle. And many now suspected that Ito was brewing on unfermented ground, because of his leniency and sometimes intolerant style of umpiring.

Most noticeable at Ito Parks and Fields was this special appearance of **BARNUM-BAILEY** and the **RINGLEY BROTHERS.** They were all there and on display with all their clowns. **The CIRCUS had come full circle and all the stars were doing their trampoline acts.** Some were inside and others were outside Ito Parks and Fields. Even the jurors had gotten into the acrobatics—tumbling along with <u>THE GREATEST SHOW ON EARTH.</u> And their exercise of combined strength against the absolute power of Lance Ito's Empire was, by all measurements, more than futile.

MUTINY ON THE BOUNTY is a well thought-out phrase for what happened last week. Jurors wanted to be heard by Ito. The only way they were to be heard was to boycott Ito's Playing Fields. They did and it was effective. He finally listened to the juror's problems and complaints, and gave out additional instructions to all counselors. That will probably not be enough for the loyal sequestered few. Ito had put on a tough act, got his game moving at a better pace, but it is expected to dwindle, given time. In other words, it's not his nature to be consistently tough-minded on his playing field with the players.

Today, Mazzola wasn't forthcoming and when you're not forthcoming on this field and you're a Prosecution witness, this Defense will make you appear a liar and in some ways you will be—if you don't have your story straight.

It started to be like pulling teeth for the now famed Neufeld. In his cross examination with Mazzola, she seemed to be claming-up with a tight mouth. She was starting to favor Fung and his mannerism of responses as a witness. That wasn't good for her or the Prosecution.

At some point, you had to think this trial was a microcosm of what's wrong with our country and this society. We leave our values at home when we need to 'fit the bill.' We follow our assumed friends and become formalist to their habits—if it means fitting in. That type becomes our role models. And usually, we are not that person at all, but we somehow give that perception—very much like how youngsters are sometimes perceived.

(April 26, 1995)

NEUFELD, MAZZOLA and back again to HANK GOLDBERG, the Prosecution; this was today's court action. Mazzola was failing the prosecution with Neufeld's cross-examination as Goldberg finished out the day, trying to rehabilitate her credibility. It will never happen, but don't say, 'I told you so.'

(April 27, 1995)

Today, Criminal-list Andrea Mazzola admits altering testimony in the Orenthal Games. **"Back in August of 1994, I was under the assumption that I put my initials on the envelope and I was WRONG,"** she said. [Just think how this will sound in the Defense's closing statement.] She was referring to a sample, which had the initials of her supervisor Dennis Fung on them.

Neufeld asked her, "Would you agree that without proper documentation, it's easy for someone to tamper with the samples."

Mazzola—now beaten down—said, "Yes."

This admission came at the end of several days of tedious testimony from her.

Jurors had snapped to attention on Thursday when this testimony came to light. She was admitting that she had changed testimony about the evidence that was collected by her and her department. **She had flip-flopped.** In fact, while her probationary period was on its hourglass, Mazzola had collected most of the blood evidence herself—bad girl. Because this gave the Defense a powerful illustration of its claims that evidence tampering and sloppiness had taken place and perhaps a testo-lying had also. At best, evidence had been handled by an amateur. The Defense showed video tapes to support this claim. In the Defense's mind, this issue could render most, if not all of the collection of sample testing meaningless.

(April 28, 1995)

It was quiet time at Ito Parks and Fields. Ito closed down the field in keeping with a promise made many moons ago to Johnnie Cochran. Cochran will be on a personal mission, perhaps a family reunion or something.

FIFTEENTH WEEK

(May 1, 1995)

Another juror was severed and replaced today. Only five alternates left. **LET THE GAMES BEGIN!**—Again, and again—To dwindle.

Gregory Matheson, Chief Forensic Chemist & Blood Analyst and LAPD Clinic DNA supervisor, linked Orenthal's blood characteristics to the Bundy crime scene last July 7, 1994. **His testimony was to be incriminating.** This had been the Prosecution's right-angle that brought the accused to trial. Well done.

Hank Goldberg is giving Matheson an easy go of it in his direct today. It appears that it's a good day—more reposed for many and Matheson is a good Prosecution witness. Here is a metaphor, in the form of a poem.

The west wind had caught Goldberg's sail
His wave seemed as smooth as silk.
His runner is on course, like a sure riding horse
But his sailing may not be as smooth as his whiff.

Clarence G. Hanley

There's little to none with his navigation.
And none to naught with this witness
But, I'm sure and I don't think we can ignore.
Defense is far from treating him like a kitten.

*   *   *

I can't deny the fact that Goldberg presents a somber aura. Matheson didn't make the atmosphere any better—both being located on the same turf, as it were. So, wake me when it's over, as Hank Goldberg continues to use experts to defend prior Prosecution witnesses against their inequities.

Didn't you notice, most of the courtroom spectators have already gone (to sleep, I mean) home. Ito Parks and Fields are nearly empty and there has been no interest and no circus today. There have been few hits, many errors, some runs and more players on deck. This game isn't near over yet.

(May 2, 1995)

Meticulously, Hank Goldberg tries to cover every anticipated area he thought the Defense might get into. He was playing their game and not his own. I know that every time you try to play another man's game, you will never have all the pieces in their proper place. Will Goldberg have all the pieces to play the Defense's game? I doubt he will, but we'll see.

(May 3, 1995)

Robert Blasier, a DNA specialist for the defense, resumed his cross examination from yesterday with Gregory Matheson, Chief of Forensics, for the LAPD. Blasier seems to be verbally juggling along with a log of questions he needed answered for defensive closing statements, or their DNA experts later on, either or both. Lawyers before had entered into sort-of-an accounting dialogue, resulting in a reasonable story. Jurors had been able to follow this line of questioning with some clarity. I'm not sure with Blasier. I think his information gathering has a proper place though. Slowly, but surely, he's raising some interesting issues—issues that continue to linger in the minds of many viewers and followers of this trial. **Was the collection of evidence contaminated?** What are those possibilities? That's what his seemingly fishing expedition was all about. I think he's getting there.

(May 4, 1995)

Blasier, of the Defense, continues to hone in on additional mishandling of evidence and scientific testimony. Chief Matheson, the chemist of forensics for the LAPD, verified each mishap. Some mishaps he approved of in terms of **common practice. The Defense's angle is to disapprove all inequities as malpractice.**

Blasier's strategy also, was to demonstrate how the blood samples tested for blood types, had bordered on malpractice; that is, when one test comes back improperly done, that diminishes its properties and thus its results. This had been a Catch-22 for the Prosecution. It is their viewpoint, but the Defense seem to have them on both counts regarding the **B-Type blood found under Nicole's fingernails.** If they say it's a B-Type, it will not belong to any one of these three—Nicole, Ron, nor Orenthal. **If a B-Type was actually found, and was a degraded Type, then the Forensics Chiefs science would have failed.**

The Defense had to struggle with foundation, before getting the above testimony in, through Matheson.

Blasier also alleged **E.D.T.A;** (a substance used to preserve blood samples) was found in some of the collection of Orenthal's blood. This will be one of the ultimate holes punched in the Prosecution's case. Cochran's opening statement now comes full circle—**COMPROMISE, CORRUPTION, and/ or CONTAMINATION.** The Prosecution can't seem to get around at least one of these for something better than a hung jury. This will be the '**Coup de Grace'**—the blow that brings death to the Prosecutions case—and finally, another waste of taxpayer's dough. But eventually, they will become better agents of the state, after several mess-ups. When he rested his case on this issue, Blasier had skillfully woven together that there was blood missing from the valve of blood taken from Orenthal. There was a possible planting of evidence having taken place and this means Orenthal was framed.

(May 5, 1995)

Hank Goldberg is again walking on thin ice with hypothetical(s) before the jurors and Ito. He went over-board, however, and could be sanctioned for putting the jurors to sleep, as even indicated by Referee Ito, but moreover, because he had not adhered to Ito's admonishment. Ito was specific when he indicated to Goldberg—"enough!" Ito finally left the field of play (his courtroom that is), in an effort to give Goldberg a chance to cool his heels. Goldberg had been trying to bandage Matheson's wounds with hypothetical(s), but he went overboard with E.D.T.A. hearsay.

When Blasier re-crossed and examined, Matheson's Code of Ethics as a scientist came into question. The Defense once again rested its case.

Hank Goldberg came back with a re-re-redirect and a pack of bandages to administer a quick first aid job—after his witness had made a bad slide into home plate with a miserable landing. The aid will probably be a short remedy in the minds of the jurors.

SIXTEENTH WEEK

(May 8, 1995)

We heard brief testimony from Bernie Douroux, a tow-truck driver, who hauled Orenthal's Ford Bronco from his home to the police headquarters the day after the homicide. He said he didn't notice any blood stains, but hadn't opened the locked vehicle. Douroux said he left the Bronco unattended for about three minutes while he looked for a detective.

Doctor Robin Cotton, Ph.D. and Lab Director for Cellmark Laboratories of Maryland, was questioned by George W. Clark of the Prosecution. They were like teachers giving their students, jurors and audience, a good basic understanding of DNA.

Defense seems to have little or no problem with this angle and objected little-to-none with this expected three day extension testimony. The Dream Teams testimony remained the same—CONTAMINATION, COMPROMISE, and CORRUPTION. Some of this angle will not go away, and some legal DOUBT will inevitably remain with this jury, I'm sure of it.

"DNA," Dr. Cotton said, "is exactly the same (99%) in all of us and is used for each one's identification. Twins were 100%. What makes the rest of our make-up different is that less than 1% DNA will map a difference in each of us." This was the most critical part of the State's case against Simpson as the biochemist explained the ABC's of DNA. She had waited for at least three days to reveal whether Orenthal's genetic fingerprints linked him to the double homicide. She used charts and drawings to explain how genes passed to a child from mother and father and how it formed the genetic blueprint of ones physical and mental make-up.

"If a blueprint contains all information on how to build a house," she told jurors, "the DNA contains information on how to build you." The prosecution and this specialist were using elementary metaphors. The specialist said, "DNA has four basic components. They are referred to as bases, spelled b-a-s-e-s, so there are four bases that make up the entire DNA. They have the names ADENINE, GUANINE, THYMINE, and CYTOSINE. And they are abbreviated . . . just by their first letter, A, T. G. and C. These four bases are the DNA alphabet. It's just like if you look at the English alphabet, it has 26 letters. And you can put those letters together to make words, which in turn make sentences, which in turn makes paragraphs."

Most jurors appeared to pay close attention, keeping their eyes on the charts being displayed. A few took notes. Now, keep in mind it will take every juror to get a conviction, or there will be a hung jury (or otherwise an acquittal). The Judge will instruct each juror to bring back one or the other. The jurors' comprehension and conception of DNA testing is vital to the Prosecution. It is expected to put the defendant at the scene of the homicide and thus convict him of this crime.

Give Dr. Cotton high marks for her thoroughness and clear delivery. Again, her explanations are crucial to whether jurors accept DNA evidence. I think some will, some will want too, and others will receive it as vague and not yet fully understood. Their mentalities will not be ready for this relatively new science.

Bewildered or not, the jury will sooner or later, labor this washed-up testimony toward a verdict. Also, when that time comes, they will possibly be put on notice, by the Defense, that Cellmark has a vested interest in this Trial of the Century. Their accepted version of DNA in this well-advertised trial will surge their business straight to the top. A larger portion of their income is currently derived from this line of their business, making this case of SPECIAL INTEREST to their company. Their mother company in England, Cellmark of England, does very little of this kind of DNA testing, making their bottom line here in the States of considerable importance toward corporate revenues.

(May 9, 1995)

A second day commences with this crash course in DNA Molecular Biology Television Class, by Dr. Robin Cotton. We are all learning a lot. Our mental digestive systems may be a little bit slow in reception, not to mention contamination, but we're getting some of it. For those thinkers who are not scientists, one logical thought hangs in the balance for some thinkers. When you have a pattern of bands that match and are now aimed at conviction, should we now agree that this Science of Biology has come full circle? Has it advanced far enough to tell us both pro and con? Some say no! Many believe that we don't yet have it all with this science, and I agree. So, the question remains, are we far enough along to convict, as well as to exonerate an alleged guilt? Yes, or no, will be a bothersome question and answer for many.

Who else's blood is on the steering wheel of the Bronco? Whose blood is under Ron Goldman's shoes? Whose blood is under Nicole's fingernails? That's what the Dream Team Defense Machine will be asking of this trail of blood and of this Prosecution. The Prosecution will continue to say that the blood trail speaks for itself. The Defense will also ask the Prosecution to show motive.

Clarence G. Hanley

(May 10, 1995)

The word overkill, by these lawyers, can hardly be stated enough. That's what makes this 'The Trial of the Century.' Overkill on both sides, says the media. And, I say, overkill with this media show, also. To paraphrase Shakespeare, everything adds up to being a media show—with the stage being the world. He says, "Out, out, brief candle, life is but a walking shadow. A poor player (witness, or lawyer) who struts and frets his hour on the stage and then is heard no more, is a story told by a signifying media." I think 'media' was what Shakespeare meant to say. I'll look it up later on, but, meanwhile the media word fills up that space for the time being—until I get the right 'monkey' word. And . . . as with each of us, "THE ENTIRE WORLD IS A STAGE." The players—well . . . we are being played upon.

Dr. Robin Cotton continued today with her re-pleat demonstration of DNA. She had been the great teacher, her audience had been her great class, and television had been her great classroom. We all had learned something about this new science and we still had some (few to many) questions for the teacher. Also, Cellmark has no independent proficiency testing for their own rights and wrong. In other words, no one monitors them for clinical practices and behaviors. No one is testing them and they have made some big boo-boos in their past—in 1988 and 1989, especially.

Culprits and wrongdoers are the focus of the Defense. As it has always been with the Defense, Prosecution's information will have its share of discrepancies. There are Portions of Prosecution's text and discrepancies in some of their books. They have problems with many of their authors, and some shortcomings with all of their teachers. This is the Defense's focus. This theorem will continue to be a part of the Defense's theory, as Peter Neufeld cross examined Dr. Cotton about some of her company's noticeable past faults. Presently, as with this DNA, and future, as in, "Will you be doing it differently in some of the testing areas" a question put to Cotton, by Neufeld). When the defense seeks the above information, they usually find it. When they knock, doors open. When they ask, they most likely receive—some favorable information that will be helpful to the defense of Orenthal. It has happened before; it will happen again. Believe me.

(May 11, 1995)

Yesterday, Dr. Robin Cotton led the jurors down a blood trail pointing toward Simpson. "It was his blood," she said. She was talking about a few drops. "Planted," the Defense will say.

Today, jurors will look at Prosecution evidence, their X-Ray copies (radiographs) under a well-lit board. Woody Clark, for the Prosecution, continues to be meticulous in his direction. And, at this point, if you have been swinging like a pendulum in your choice of guilt or innocence, there is little doubt Orenthal Simpson has thrown the 'killer ball.' For four days the Prosecution's cup had runneth over with hits, runs, little or no errors and no competition with their DNA testing, (Orenthal's DNA). Dr. Robin Cotton went as far as to say, "There is simply no other DNA that will match the blood found at Bundy. It belongs to the defendant."

The overall question now hangs in the balance. Is he guilty? Or, is this a lynching with a scientific rope—CONTAMINATED with CORRUPTIONS and COMPROMISES. Will the blood trail matter, or will this trial call for a deeper thought from jurors? Your guess is as good as mine.

As the Prosecution continued on with their direct, it has to be said, they had done a superb job in their presentation. It seemed, by now, the command had been given to build the hanging gallows and to order invitations—and to let the final ceremonies begin.

We had been taught quite a lot in this field of science, by Dr. Cotton. DNA—surely, the science of the future, which is where THIS jury might very well put it, that is . . . in the future.

When it was time for Neufeld to cross examine this expert witness, he wanted to make her his own witness. But he couldn't seem to get his hypothetical together today. Ito was having a hard time giving him much leeway to do so. Peter Neufeld wanted to show what had happened early on, before Dr. Cotton or her Cellmark Laboratories had came into this homicide case. He wanted to paint a portrait of CONTAMINATION, along with a degree of COMPROMISE and CORRUPTION. Can he stay this course? Can he maintain this task? Let's wait and see.

The fury of Ito and his gavel cost Neufeld and Woody Clark $250 each. Neufeld tried to present a letter before the court, one that had never been published. George Woody Clark had tried to object, but the objection came after the parliamentary gavel of Ito and after he had sustained both to a ruling he wanted to give. The parliamentary procedure simply got a little out of hand, a bit messy and somewhat confused. And because Referee Ito had this great need to self-censor the job he wasn't doing, he issued sanctions to both attorneys.

As they both tried to borrow and beg for their fees, Ito reminded each that this was a personal sanction—meaning they each had to pay it themselves. I noticed Darden lending cash to Clark for his sanction fees, and other Defense attorneys were trying to lend Neufeld his fees in those moments before Ito reminded them both that this was a personal sanction. It perhaps caused Neufeld to be leery of where his fees came from, so he wrote a personal check to the Court Clerk. So smile if you can, because . . . .

ROUND AND ROUND AND ROUND WE GO

WHERE THIS TRIAL WILL STOP

NO ONE REALLY KNOWS.

NOT US, NOT YOU

THAT WOULD HARDLY DO

WE CAN'T CIRCUMVENT THE FACTS

WE MUST ALL REMAIN MEDIA FOOLS.

*   *   *

(May 12, 1995)

Peter Neufeld continued to hammer away at Dr. Cotton's opinions about DNA. His attacks have not gone without several hand slap pings by Ito. You would think Neufeld would be angry by now, but he hasn't shown that he is. In fact, he is probably gaining a great deal of respect with this jury for his patience with Ito's new (re-established) ways. He's been using his gavel rather heavy-handedly in my opinion. He is being watched by all, as his display of adamant censure might turn out to be his worst nightmare. Perhaps we might see another mutiny on his bounty, or perhaps a backlash will be aimed at his new attitude. That aim can only hurt the Prosecution.

When Neufeld is given some leeway in his cross, he seems to make some headway for his team. Ito has a way of cutting him off which appears unfair to some media-maniacs. But if they can see it, rest assured that the jurors are well aware of this unfair display. Perhaps, when it is time to hear his final instruction for a ruling on this case, some jurors will harbor his newfound attitude to be paid-in-kind. I'm sure that he has lost control of this jury, but that occurred long ago.

What will happen when the Defense finally puts its case on with its witnesses? We will see. Many of us are in slumber. This science has put us there. Ito will wake some of us when it's over. Because for now, it looks like Orenthal's going to stay behind bars—until the flow of revenues dwindles to a slow pour. Only then, will this trial begin to dry up to clarity of wisdom and civility for many. Because, as many realized, this trial is about capitalism, jobs, revenues, media, lawyers and judges. But, what about the homicide, I hollered . . . *What about the homicide?* **What about the homicide?** *They didn't hear me I suppose—as if I were asleep, or was I dreaming.*

SEVENTEENTH WEEK

(May 15, 1995)

If and when Peter Neufeld made any headway on behalf of the Defense, Ito made sure that his headway was hard fought. Even Dr. Cotton, the Prosecutions star witness, saw a need to help Neufeld in his cross-examination. She would simply give a summation in some of her responses to help him with some of his questions that were almost for sure to be objected to and sustained by Ito if Newfeld had ask the question himself. As a professor, Dr. Robin Cotton was like an elementary school teacher and Neufeld her favorite student. She would smile at times when she seemed to know what he was getting at, when he had been sustained. So sometimes, she would simply summate in her next answer, to the question before thus helping him with his earlier question. As the professorial type, she seemed to understand the need to project some sympathy his way. Ito was meanwhile paving a most rocky road for him. He was sustaining his questions at the drop of a hat and with every possible chance he had. He just didn't want Neufeld to open any roads of provocation to new evidence. Instead, he wanted Neufeld to finish his line of questioning and go back to Brooklyn.

Will statistics prove this defendant guilty beyond a reasonable doubt? Have there been too many trees in this forest of DNA evidence? Is this science generally adept when it's not being specifically flawed—Questions and more questions.

The Defense echoed that Cellmark made big mistakes in 1988 and 1989 mistakenly crossing their tests. The other big problem they had then and continued to have now, was that they didn't do efficiency, or blind tests. With that, once again, the Defense suggested they just might be making another big mistake. Furthermore, the Defense was saying, can this science be relied upon in this trial for something other than just assumptions—assumptions that have been derived from a large database of minutes and numbers?

When it was all said and done, it was found that the Prosecution's statistics had been extrapolated from a database of only two hundred Afro-Americans, all from one location.

(May 16, 1995)

Harmon of the Prosecution and Gary Sims, D.O.J. Forensics Scientist and Criminal-list of the California Department of Justice, produced a long verbal display of Simpson's dark socks. They were found in the middle of the bedroom floor of the defendant's meticulously kept home. Doubtful, some have said. But the Prosecution felt they were onto something in dealing with those infamous, invisible blood stained socks—a stain that was found some weeks later.

Saturated with old news and the Prosecution wanting to expound even further, in this area, frustration set in with the law-embattled Ito. Dismayed, but holding his composure, he simply asked Harmon to move on to another area, away from this DNA/sock business.

LET'S SET THE RECORD STRAIGHT. Satire of this type can sometimes be contrary, but satire of this type can also be good. The question remains: IS THE SYSTEM BROKEN? Even if only partly broken, let's begin to try and fix it. We can learn a lot from this trial.

(May 17, 1995)

Today, the odds continue to stack up against Orenthal, as the Prosecutor's Forensics Expert from the D.O.J., Gary Sims, nails him to a CROSS. **The Defense's CROSS examiner, Barry Scheck, will be PALLBEARER of the CROSS. And with every effort, Scheck will try to CROWBAR most every NAIL from Orenthal's CROSS—perhaps only to save each to later NAIL Prosecution to their own COFFINS.** In other words, it doesn't look very good for Orenthal right now, the pundits are saying. And they know everything, even before the Defense comes up to bat.

One thing to remember, the Defense has THEIR case to put on, yet. And they're simply looking for a REASONABLE DOUBT. They will surely get reasonable doubt if they can show these jurors Orenthal had absolutely nothing to do with starting the EBOLA VIRUS (the African killer plague). Instead, they will project the LAPD/CRIMINALIST as having possibly started such a famine in their mishandling of DNA.

(May 18, 1995)

Undoing the damage the Prosecution has done to Orenthal with expert witnesses will not be easy. But, Scheck went to work on Gary Sims today, in an effort to make him the Defenses witness, and to perhaps support their contamination theory.

(May 19, 1995)

Today I watched Barry Scheck almost mechanically go up to Gary Sims, scientifically reach over his head and swing the Prosecution pendulum back to the Defense's court. Earlier in the day, he had cast a shadow on doubts with the **LAPD COLLECTION and HANDLING** of evidence. He still had further to go. He'll do that Monday.

And guess what? I could understand most of his logic. He, in essence, became the teacher that **Dr. Robin Cotton** had been.

This game is far from over. **So hold on to your raffle tickets, any number can yet be drawn from this brewer's distillery.** And keep your seats too, playoff tickets will be hard to find. There's going to be a sellout. **Scalpers will continue eyeballing the pendulum,** so watch your heads and be careful what you buy, and don't use you credit cards—they might incriminate you before this charade is over.

Many media types will also be wholesaling their side-shows. Some will drop ship mail-orders and package plans. Others will sell over-the-counter pick-ups. **There will be VISA and MASTER plans.** Many will have **DISCOVERY** deals, and yet others **AMERICAN EXPRESS.**

Rest assured the scalpers will remain a part of these games at Ito Parks and Fields. And if this piece is not clearly understood, simply call your local news reporter. They will gladly give you the names of each of their **PEN SCALPERS, their STORY SELLERS,** I mean storytellers. When you call be aggressive and don't give up. Make sure you get a sample of everyone's **PEN MAN SHIP.**

EIGHTEENTH WEEK

(May 22, 1995)

Last Friday, when Barry Scheck closed out the day, he asked Gary Sims a **musical chime** (it sounded like a chime to me). "Isn't it fair to say, you don't know **HOW** and you don't know **WHEN** that blood got on the sock, isn't it sir?" Sims hummed, "**NO-O-O!**" (No sir, I don't.")

(May 23, 1995)

PROSECUTION has spared no expense in this case. Today, Rock Harmon and another one of their witnesses demonstrated strong evidence and it just kept coming. They had an expert witness here, an expert witness there; they had an expert, expert, expert witness everywhere. They seemed to swallow up this Dream Team in experts, almost devouring their theory of **COMPROMISE, CORRUPTION, or CONTAMINATION.**

Rock Harmon had continued to beat the dead horse to another death with experts. It all seemed **JURASSIC** in Ito's **PARK.** But it all remained questionable to me in this first merry-go-round. Dr. Robin Cotton had given me a good elementary educational base. I still had miles to go, while trying to be equitable. It wasn't easy, but I did feel like I had gotten an idea about this (DNA) stuff from Dr. Cotton.

It could have been Interesting to me today, however IT-IS-NOT. In fact, I can hardly keep count of the **winks, the winks, the winks**. What I am trying to say is that I can hardly count the winks I have contributed to this segment of the trial. Before, and early on, I had been wide eyed and bushy-tailed. I had been in the mode of helping this jury figure out this homicide. My intention was to do it long before this case would be handed to them for a verdict. However, all this DNA stuff has taken some of the wind out of my sails. The winks seem to come ever so closely now. Oh, well! This trial can't wait; it must go on. I must get back to my purpose—back to the grind. It must go on. 'Try to remember,' I kept telling myself, 'try to remember once again—the story, the story,' this is the Trial of the Century and there are yet miles to go. This trial must go on, it must go on, it must, it must . . . .

AWAKENING FROM SOMNOLENCE

Continue from chapter one . . . .

. . . The girl, she was saying, "I SAW IT, I SAW IT ALL."

"Wow!" I said to myself. Had she?

And now awake, and . . . .

By this time and after listening to her monologue for a period of time, I wasn't sure whether I had received the entire story she wanted to tell me. So, I simply asked the big question, "Who were the men? And who did it?" I was even more curious now. I wanted to know the crux of this story.

Marci responded, "The guy with the voice from the police station where his wife works, I'm convinced now, was the Judge. The last guy arriving at the homicide scene was the detective—Fuhrman. The guy who said, 'Oh my God!' is on trial—Mr. Simpson. The latter two guys who ran—were foreigners. I think they actually did the crime—who knows. The guy before that, who had ran across the street and seemed confused, he was that lawyer on the Defense, the dark one, Afro-American, or maybe the Jewish one with the Italian last name—he was dark too. The one before that was the dark lawyer on the Prosecution's team. They all seem to have their faults in this troublesome case," she noted. "They were all guilty of something."

As she seemed to calm her now-emotional state of mind, she seemed to also reach back in her thoughts and summoned the question, "Did I tell you my full name yet?"

I said, "No! You did not."

"I'm Marci Clark," she replied. "I want to write a book."

And again, faintly she said, "I SAW IT ALL." Then she seems to demonstrate her confusion as her voice grew fainter, saying, "I saw it all, I . . . saw it all, it all, I think, I . . . I . . . saw . . . saw it . . . all . . . ."

LATER

And, in case you didn't notice, this DNA part of the trial laid me to rest. <u>Somnolence</u> came upon me unknowingly and many others undoubtedly blinked and winked an eye or two also. I just couldn't resist the **torpid journey into a theta state** of unconsciousness as **Marci told me her story in my dream**. There were parts of the trial that left many in slumber. This happened to a great number of people, including myself. And what a dream! <u>It was my dream</u>.

But, I hadn't become Rip Van Winkle. **When I finally awoke,** I knew even less than I thought I knew while I was awake and writing this piece—it *had become AN ODE TO SATIRE.* The protagonist in **my dream** may not have had her finger on the exact pulse of this trial, but her story could be a principal one.

You see, this *TRIAL OF THE CENTURY* had accumulated far too many theories. Many have agreed that most any crime scenario would be just as good as all others that were floating around. But, I really think we would all be much better off if we would just let the system take its course in these cases—absent of the pundits' special biases. If we really want to believe in our system's jurisprudence and help it work to maximum, then, we have to believe, *THIS MAN WAS INNOCENT UNTIL PROVEN GUILTY* by our justice system. A large percentage of Americans did not do that. They were lured by their biases, the media and all of its commentators.

As the jurors continued to hear the circumstantial evidence being presented and before my lapse of conscious time, the trial had still a ways to go. The trial was not even half through yet. For one thing, the Defense had not yet put on its case. *Also, jurors continued to dwindle—some had been thrown off. Three or four alternates were left by now.* And, before I fell asleep, I wondered if the jury was as bewildered as me by the DNA presentation. I'll *admit, I have appeared biased toward the judicial system. My intention was to remain neutral, and in my heart of hearts I have.*

I did like the sound of THE DREAM TEAM DEFENSE MACHINE. It sounded much better to me than THE PROSECUTING HEAD HUNTERS (I made this name up you should know). When I first heard the name of the Defense, produced by one of the pundits, I immediately realized that they were considering this as a game of sorts. And that was when I wrote my first page—January, 1995. I was caught up in the frenzy by then and, like many others each day, I could not be shifted.

NOW I've turned in my flag, perhaps I should say my PEN. I probably should have never gotten in this game anyway. But this game is over for me. Most others had wished the same. Then there was Geraldo Rivera. His life seemed centered around the infamy of it all. He seemed to be learning to be a lawyer. He had been a law student before—but never got much practice as a lawyer. He was getting plenty now as a pundit.

I can't forget, however, that the case of the Prosecutions efforts will rest on CIRCUMSTANTIAL EVIDENCE. How far did that carry with the jurors? Well, I won't be biased anymore—will I? But, if you had an incident like Marci did (in my slumber) and you were now one of the jurors, then circumstantial evidence would not carry very far with you. And you can bet that many of those jurors know someone who had some unfair experiences, regardless of answers later conveyed.

Remember too, *there had been no CONFESSION, no EYE WITNESS, no MURDER WEAPON and no BLOOD STAINED CLOTHING*—other than the *belated sock stain.* There simply was no true and proven *PHYSICAL EVIDENCE*—only speculations, *hypothetical(s),* and scenarios. Do some believe there had been a *COMPROMISE* and some *CORRUPTION?* Yes! And could many individuals have been involved? Probably not! But it would only take one domino to cascade the corruption of all others and only the first or few need to know where the corrupt domino fell from.

And finally, do I believe Orenthal James Simpson did this homicide? There is no way I can know for sure, and neither does the public—without having been there. He will have to bear his own burdens—with God. But I suggest the law be followed properly. What we think we might know and believe, I think theology has given us the best answer for that judgment—*"JUDGE NOT LEST YOU BE JUDGED and VENGEANCE IS MINE, SAYETH THE LORD."* The rest should be left to our jurisprudence system, the law of the land.

SUMMARIZATION

THIRTY THREE WEEKS

(Monday September 4, 1995)

By now . . . .

The Great Lance Ito and his Empire had tumbled close to recusal. His wife, a high-ranking officer with the LAPD, had all but experienced redactation before redemption to her pedestal. The Great Umpire had cried in front of millions, saying, "I would (sic) loved my wife dearly." Each of us began to ask ourselves, "What did he mean . . . ?"

How far had we come in the TRIAL OF THE CENTURY? How far had we all come?

As my revival from slumber and somnolence is complete, and my views now seemed more clarified, most all the blood had settled by now. The pen man, his penmanship and his ink, had once again been encouraged to flow. He/I like many, could hardly believe Orenthal had done this thing. But whom . . . And who could really know—even after an acquittal, a hung jury or otherwise? Had the evidence been authenticated—after Detective Mark Fuhrman's revelation? Orenthal knew for sure. God knew. Ron and Nicole, they knew. This is all by way of saying that we the public did not know. Others, including the experts, did not know the real true facts of this case either, and many could only circumvent their circumstantial hearts, their minds and their tools.

The LAPD, on the other hand, they know what they know. In fact, the facts of each individual professional player, each now knew their position in this case—favorable, or unfavorable.

I have to express myself and say, I didn't like what I saw at the outset of the circumstances in this case. In fact, I felt like my rights were being violated when Fuhrman went over Orenthal's wall without a warrant.

So, here we are in the Thirty Second, Thirty Third and latter Weeks of the trial with new evidence; it involves Mark Fuhrman. There are two alternate jurors left now and one of those now hung by the thinnest thread. A collection of tapes from Laura Hart McKinney, a North Carolina Script Writer had evolved this case into the next node and further reinforced it as the **TRIAL OF THE CENTURY**.

Fuhrman's lies and perjuries had come full circle now. Also, Vanatter had now been demonstrated to have had a reckless disregard for the truth. Mark Fuhrman had broken the case wide open against Orenthal in testifying he found the gloves and traces of blood, then scaling the wall and finally lying in the witness box. These tapes however, had claimed the direction of his final destiny and the trial—perhaps POETIC JUSTICE. Now, he was on trial with that same society. He truly was a ROGUE COP. Perhaps there are others and he will take the rap—perhaps not. All of that will eventually have its place in history.

Wide awake now, I found that the latter weeks in the Defense's case had been momentous. They had peaked in most every instance. In many ways their case had been the summary to the trial. *I had been left with a confluence of thoughts, aftermaths, questions and other contemplations of recompense.* Because, for many the trial will go on, many will not reconcile their inquisitions—regardless of the wisdom confronting them. We will call them diehards. That type has always been a part of our society.

But, paramount in my modus cognition will be, where do we go from here as a society? Now that we have touched on our closet issues, what are our aims? What about the issues we carry around with us in our everyday lives, on our jobs, at social gatherings, at our homes? Issues we are faced with every day in our jurisprudence life—an arena that can determine freedom or incarceration to anyone's life and livelihood and sometimes life or death. The Rodney King Trial had finally let the police issue out of the bag. Many already knew about that shortcoming. The Fuhrman case, perhaps now brings that problem full circle. So . . . for those who have said this was not an LAPD Trial, or Fuhrman Trial, they were mistaken. Everyone is on trial each day of our lives—trial before God, if nothing else.

It is perhaps the main issue, because credibility always stands at the forefront. **It is the gauge, upon which we base our jurisprudence system. Orenthal will be no different.**

It's just a thought and I don't suggest its likelihood, but if Orenthal is assassinated, (civically, physically or socially) because of any person or group's deep belief against the outcome, our society will suffer. The system would have further shown its flaws. Our society will increase its measure of risk and blame. Multiplications of heated remonstrations will lead to increasing devastation.

Almost every pundit has brought his/her own biases to the playing field causing this cementation/sensation game to be played on far too many fields. That has been one of the systems biggest travesties, and perhaps our society's truest sham.

Another issue was watching the Defense draw straws each day from the **KINGDOM OF ITO**. Fairness they cried—fairness!! They would sometimes gain a feather or two in their caps to help carry their case-in-trial with some honor and a small show of fairness. And I'm not sure, but sometimes Ito's Kingdom seemed much distorted and was truly a **LEANING TOWER OF PISA**—an image he seemed destined to convey. Overall though, I intuit that he was as fair as he could be—under the circumstances. Perhaps the worse was yet to come.

There is a duty for people in authoritative positions; however they need to help bring a fraying people together—all of them—something that has never been done in the history of this society. It cannot be treated or handled as a passing fancy either. It must be heartfelt. We should be **LOVING OUR NEIGHBORS AS WE LOVE OURSELVES**, not trying to dig each others grave for more power and money.

Let me say something about this. There seemed not to have been any true search for other possible assailants: That's not an investigation, and that's a big part of what went wrong with the Prosecution's case—and many other cases in this land. The system was looking for easy problem solving—easy outs. **Could someone have been paid to be the culprit—is one other avenue not pursued?** When the case came to light and the trial was underway, it became demonstrative of where the systems heart laid and their direction of pursuit. The lighted way illuminated the biases in America. It had long past been very typical of the American way—more subtle now at this time than ever before. It had infuriated those folks who didn't want their subtle emotions out of their closets. These infuriated folks were traveling their chosen roads in their chosen vehicles. It was hard for many—as many were trying very hard to get off their winding ways. Many had not followed ones least traveled roads—as that could have made all the difference in their personal history, their country and their lives. And as it were, most were out to win their cause, at any cost. We all have always been taught such mentality since birth, to win at most any, even honorable cost. That is how this trial became secondary to guilt or innocence, on both sides. Each had his or her own agenda, as many others did also in the viewing public. Some agendas were good and honorable, and some were not.

ANOTHER SUMMARY THOUGHT—the prosecutors were Head Hunters. Those on the Defenses Team were actors. The Defense had really become endeared with the idea that they were **Protectors of the Constitution**. I really thought they were more like protectors of their fame and fortune. But, in every way, both were out to win at most any plausible cost—and that would turn out to be one of the issues. Each side had been like the gladiators they were. They each were seeking their own trophies and speaking a geldings neigh-h-h to winning at any cost. But both sides in their bid were surely playing the same horse game and each was racing for the finish line.

The complete turn-a-bout in this case came from the Eighth Week of testimony from **AN ODE TO SATIRE**. F. Lee Bailey had asked a besieging question of Mark Fuhrman, "Have you ever used the 'N' word in the last Ten Years?" Fuhrman gave an unequivocal reply, "No!" Bailey afforded him every opportunity to change his answer. Fuhrman then was asked several different ways, and answered 'No' to each. The question could have been accepted as a mistake, or a bedeviled question, for someone else. But for Fuhrman, because he had been taken off the case immediately, (because of his attitude, his gesture, his body language and what he said he had found as he jumped the wall of Orenthal's estate) his answer was a lie. Some viewers have opted not to prosecute that lie, that perjury pursued by the Defense. The defense had a right to their case. Opposing groups can sometimes find themselves in a bias mode when their modus operandi is trampled on, or maybe they could care less about the process or the system. They simply wanted Orenthal's head on a platter at any cost. They are why this system will continue to have major flaws.

Back during the Eighth Week of testimony, Fuhrman had been dishonest. He had also been a bit to **relish** as a cop. But now, what will become of his lack of honor? He is now dishonored by many who had loved him before for his gallantry against the lawyering of the famous F. Lee Bailey. Bailey had been the famed attorney who inspired Doctor Sam Sheppard's case THE FUGITIVE. It later became the long running television series. Many decided that they simply did not like this lawyer anymore. Because now and during his cross-examination of Mark Fuhrman's testimony, they subtlety decided they liked what Fuhrman stood for. But this man could have been headed for prison. He surely was headed for an investigation.

Bailey and his brilliance of another moment-in-time had now been out to get Detective Fuhrman to say in the court of jurisprudence the now infamous word 'NO' to having said the 'N Word' at another course in time and nothing considerably to do with the trial itself accept to show that this man was a liar. So Bailey had accomplished his goal—and some. F. Lee Bailey had been the case-maker, or the case-breaker, accorded to the side of the playing field you were on. He had savored THE TRIAL OF THE CENTURY for the Defense, with an air of sour-to-sweet aroma—a characteristic that had not been too pleasant for the Defense down the Prosecution's stretch in proposing DNA.

So there will be diehards who will never believe Fuhrman could have planted this evidence against Orenthal. Most of them will be from Missouri, the show-me-state (a metaphor). For them, this liar, this perjurer, only did what they (the viewers) had been told he did, short of the full story by the Prosecution. This was their case-in-trial, you should know. Even then—this group being spoon-feed—were perhaps improperly focused. The Prosecution knew the real character of this man before he became a witness. A star witness he was and they didn't tell a soul. To this diehard group, the tapes meant one thing—and the DNA meant another. They could hardly visualize the extent this man could or would go to embrace his cause before his retirement.

Then there is MAW, Men against Women—what a thought, what a purpose and what a man? But this is the sort of person Mark Fuhrman had become.

In 1983, Fuhrman's files—as indicate by the media—that he was trying to tell his employers something about himself. He was saying, I can't take it anymore. He didn't like **Niggers and Chinks**. His employer didn't listen. They would not award him disability. Instead, they turned a deaf ear. Perhaps, then, he felt an open range to act as he was pleased too. Perhaps he did, I don't know.

The **CHRISTOPHER COMMISSION** had **proven its case.** There were **ROGUE COPS** on the **LAPD** force. The Simpson Trial had been its best barometer—following **Rodney King**.

So, while the daily activities of this court had dwindled to an end, this trial was not yet over, not by a long shot—and here's why. While many have raised the flagship of **F. Lee Bailey as a Gold Medal Winner**, as an angel of grace, this trial and its personalities will have become this society's impasse. In many ways it will be their '**a coup de grace**'. While some will hold Bailey a traitor, others will maximize his net worth in a more positive way. Neither group will own up to being a color bias society, because they will not be able to justify that atmosphere. They will follow the flow as a closet case. It's our way of life in America, so Life will go on. We will remember in our exchanges of thoughts, the signs of the times and many will say . . . .

He was some Football star. He was my champion in his hey day. In time, these words would have been echoed in many forms and fashions. They would have been speaking of Orenthal James Simpson. They would have been speaking about his brief moment-in-time.

Then, there will be those who will remember that they wanted this O.J. guy hung-up and strung-out to dry and that they had been defied by the likes of Bailey. They are not exactly sure why they would have wanted this thing, but one thing for sure; it was going to make them feel better. Misconception will always be some people's forte. It's apropos for them with certain peer groups. For that crew, they are like the old **Roman Empire Society** and their gaming arenas. Where it was thumbs down to their champions, if it was to satisfy their whims, their misconceptions—that day. They didn't care about a poor soul. "Defile him, they will say! He is filthy! He was the perpetrator! He was the killer! He abused his wife! If he abused his wife, he must be guilty of the homicide." If they were not at the crime scene this will be their misconceptions. Each in their most proclaimed Christian way will stand tall with their thumbs drawn, pointedly toward the ground. With fiery eyes, they would have closed the books on a case in time.

There is more **FOOD FOR THOUGHT**. It is so easy to abuse your brother, your sister, your mom, your dad and of course your wife, when finally each will die in his or her own unexplained way. And yes! Perhaps we have already abused them, perhaps even already shortened their lives. Each of us has done that in our own un-acknowledged and un-explained way. Its human nature to demonstrate one's weaker side and we all shun admit tingly that we have.

So . . . once again, did Orenthal slaughter Nicole and Ron? And once again, that is not our call. But it all shall be opined in the minds of the beholder however, when yet again . . . F. Lee Bailey would have inspired a rendition for a society's next media soap opera, or media mini series or simply the Inquirer. Each of us will once again have been a player and yet again only in the shadows of the game itself. Once again, Shakespeare will have echoed a well-rehearsed reverberation—from his grave. "OUT, OUT BRIEF CANDLE. LIFE'S BUT A WALKING SHADOW—A POOR PLAYER THAT STRUTS AND FRETS HIS HOUR UPON THE STAGE, AND THEN IS HEARD NO MORE, IS A TALE TOLD BY AN IDIOT, FULL OF SOUND AND FURY, SIGNIFYING NOTHING."

Before moving on, we give respect to all who have departed before and after the trial—and now the *FINAL ODE*.

THE FINAL ODE

THE ACCUSED HAD RAISED BOTH HANDS AND
OPENED HIS GLOVED FIST
PROCLAIMING ARTHRITIS WOULD EXONERATE HIM
FROM ALL THIS
BUT WHEN ALL WAS FINAL AND THE VERDICT WAS IN
RHETORICAL BELLOWS RANG OUT AGAIN, and Again
TAKE THE MONEY WAS SAID, TAKE HIS FAME
HOW SAD CRIED THE ACCUSED, IT'S A CAPITALIST
GAME
PROCLAIMING THE TIME WOULD COME
AND LIKEWISE THE TIME WOULD GO
THE GAME BEING PLAYED
WOULD HAUNT OTHERS ALSO

SOMEHOW, REMEMBERING A FORGIVING SAVIOR
WAS ON A TALL MOUNTAIN SIDE
HAD VIEWED THE LAND
AS THE DEVIL HAUNTED HIM WITH SIGHS
I OWN IT ALL
WAS THE DEVILS POMPOUS CRY
AND I'LL GIVE IT TO YOU
IF YOU'LL COME OVER TO MY SIDE
JUST PROMISE YOUR SOUL
ASSURING THERE WOULD BE MUCH MORE
AND I'LL GIVE IT ALL
WAS THE DEVILS ENCORE

Clarence G. Hanley

I'LL GIVE YOU GREAT HONORS
AND WORLDLY PRIDE
JUST FOLLOW ME OVER
COME OVER TO MY SIDE

AND THEN THERE WAS ATTORNEY BAILEY
NEVER TO FORGET HIS BELOVED FRIEND
HATE CROPPED BETWEEN THE TWO
CAUSING ONE TO TURN THE OTHER IN

SO BAILEY WENT TO JAIL
THE GOVERNMENT SAID HE DID THEM WRONG
SOMETHING ABOUT DRUG MONEY
AND WHEN THEY CAME BACK, IT WAS GONE.

AND NOW A FIGHT WAS BREWING
IT WAS OVER THE CRIMINALS MONEY
THE CONFLICT SEEMED UNENDING
AND THE MASSES THOUGHT IT WAS FUNNY.

IT SEEMED A SAME OLD SONG
AGAIN BEING PLAYED OUT-OF-TUNE
THE DEVIL AGAIN WAS WINNING
JUST CAN'T BEAT THAT OLD COON.

THE GOVERNMENT WANTED THE MONEY
WHICH DIDN'T NECESSARILY BELONG TO THEM
BUT WAS CONTROLLED BY BAILEY AS THE CRIMINAL'S
LAWYER
HE WAS NOW BEING PORTRAYED A MIME.

THE GOVERNMENT WITHOUT A CONTRACT
CONTENDED OVER AND OVER AGAIN
IT JUST DID NOT BELONG TO THE HOLDER
IT JUST DID NOT BELONG TO HIM.

WHEN FINALLY THE WORLD,
ONCE AGAIN, ALL SEEMED AT ODDS
NO FORGIVENESS FOR MANY
THEY ALL SEEMED ROOTED IN SOD
OTHERS HAD AIMS TOO
THEY RAISED FELINE ARMIES
FORGIVENESS FOR THEM
SEEMED TOO MUCH LIKE HARMONY

ALAS, DARDEN AND CLARK
THEY BOTH GOT SEMI RICH
THEIR LOVE PLANS AND HATE GAMES
HAD THE MASSES MINDFULLY MIXED
DARDEN SEEMED TO HATE O.J.
CLARK WAS YET TO BE ASSESSED
THE DOUGH THESE PUBLIC SERVANTS HAD ACQUIRED
WAS CAUSING A POLITICAL MESS

AND WHAT MAY WE GATHER OR CAN WE LEARN FROM
ALL THIS
IS IT A LAND OF CHAOS, PERHAPS ENDOWED TOWARD
ABYSS
ARE WE ALL LOVE PARTNERS AND WORLDLY
CAPITAL-LIST
THE LAND, THE MONEY, ARE THEY PRODUCERS OF
MISFITS

Clarence G. Hanley

SO . . . BEDEVIL, THIS DEVIL, THE DEVILISH ONES WILL
CRY
COME OVER, COME ON OVER—OVER TO OUR SIDE
A THIRD TRIAL WAS HELD
SOME SAY DESIGNED TO DEMONSTRATE JIM CROW
JUSTICE
AS TO THE WAY THE TRIAL WAS HANDLED
SEEMED TO SOME SO VERY DISGUSTING
THE JURORS WERE SURELY MANDATED
WITH THE MEDIA GRANDFATHERED IN
COUNTRIES ACROSS THE WORLD
BEGIN TO THINK AMERICAN JUSTICE, A NATURAL SIN

FINALLY THE GAVEL HAD SIGNALED
A GESTURE THAT ALL COULD HEAR
AMERICAN JUSTICE ONCE AGAIN HAD SPOKEN
TO THOSE WHO HAD JEERED, SHALL NOW HAVE FEAR
THAT THE MASTER REMAINS
A MIGHTY PREVAILING MASTER, A BABALON PEER

DEVILS, BEDEVILED—WITH A DEVILISH CRY
COME OVER, COME OVER, OVER TO MY SIDE

BUT WHEN ALL IS DONE
AND AS THE DEVILS WILL BE DEAD
THE PROMISE WILL BE COUNTED
AND THE SEVENTH SEAL WOULD HAVE SAID
YOU HAVE BRUISED HIS HEEL
AND NOW HE HAS BRUISED YOUR HEAD
WHO IS NOW WORTHY
TO BE RAISED FROM THE DEAD

THE DENOUEMENT

PART I

The question will always be, do we have all the answers to a complex situation? Do we know all there is to know about any and everything? The answer is 'no'. Even after all the research and discovery available to us, we will not have all the answers. It is simply impossible to answer every question—psychologically, physiologically, scientifically, proactive, reactive, cognitively, and on, and on. It is impossible in any case. You react to what you have at hand.

Professionals and even I as a writer will have you believe that we have answered all of the questions—yet we keep writing, and writing, and writing—as others continue to discover new horizons, unending horizons

These are the facts of life. We push the envelope to unknown edges—perhaps this is my present aim. However, I say, not true that we have all the answers. Neither I, nor anyone can answer every question in a homicide. It is impossible. Lives are complicated beyond present understandings . . . and therein lie ones misunderstand of a full discovery. We live with a civil disposition . . . and we use present information available to us—when we have a degree of evidence. We call it as we see it, and we settle. For some small corners, that will not be enough because human lives are very complicated—changing day by day . . . beyond our meager knowledge and understanding; DNA in this case proved how little we knew at that time as well.

In other words, we don't always get it right and for the most part, we don't really know if we got it right are not. However . . . we go to bed with some comfort, accepting a fact of life and of human nature that we have done the best that we knew how.

Our denouement puts the irrelevancy and the unknown in perspective in order to make life livable and relevant. The definition of the word denouement means the final outcome of the main dramatic complication—in a literary work; or the outcome of a complex sequence of events . . . and is why we are closing with our denouement. We know a lot, yet we know very little . . . it's complicated.

For the most part this book will ask, why are the scales tipped so unbalanced in our civil display when we know a lot—yet very little? I continue to say that something has to be wrong.

Three trials had deliberated by now—the CRIMINAL, CUSTODY and CIVIL TRIAL—and yet another was on the horizon, and finally incarceration for Simpson was less of a challenge—but not the amount of time. This saga had been a staggering actuality in realizing a segment of our society had not captured the mystery and reality of the Simpson saga.

Many seem to be living in a fishbowl. Others had a rhetorical denial of unquestionable reality. Money, mixed marriage, celebrity, fame and personalities had been everyone's talking point—perhaps their mantras. This test had spurned optimum, and to no end. It seemed the real problem in our country. Race Relations, Spousal Abuse and our Criminal Justice System were spinning politically—and I am not sure which direction even yet. It has not been a positive foresight for me. All had been atmospherically charged . . . where many had become comfortable and accepting with, each of us wanted to appear personally noble in our events . . . as it were—and yet unaware as to our honest knowledge of the problems we were facing in each of our families, our country, and the world. White and Black friends alike were in denial. It was easy for each of us to chasten our heartfelt feelings about the trial. Most of us were lying to ourselves. And of course, why not, it's our protective skin in a society just waiting for one or the other to convey a thought different from his, or her own. It became very easy to chastise the other and list him or her in an opposing memory bank, as an outsider—outside of their personal views and perspectives. So, many would lie to remain a part of the in-crowd. It's was less of a hassle on their jobs and with their social groups.

Most of us were not in the same limelight as the jurors were—in the Simpson case. But many were judging. Some were praying to God—with fear—asking, "how did (they) (I) get caught up in this O.J. mess?" and passively accepting the fact that each of us were only human—yet victims.

*Simpson, otherwise, was perhaps asking himself, "How in the hell did I get caught up in this mess?" Perhaps speaking in a low monotone voice, and now besieged by his acquired place in our society and history itself. "I didn't do this thing," he had most likely uttered from time to time—**with other known incriminating thoughts however.** "The people, who said they loved me, believe I am guilty—and as guilty as guilt can be. I have tried to play fairly by the rules, not withstanding my human shortcomings, but I wouldn't kill anyone—**myself.** I honestly have a love for life and humankind—**and self.** I simply could not, would not and did not do this thing. Why am I not believed? If only I had not gone to Nicole's house the night of the homicide. And of course, those Bruno Magli' Shoes, and those photos; (??) Would the truth have really set me free of this agony I feel inside? Could I have told them I had arrived at the scene after the homicide and would they have believed me? Perhaps I will never know the answer to this question. Perhaps if I had no history of any sort of abuse with Nicole. For that matter, if I had not been a football star, or Black, or wealthy, or cunning, or crafty, or guileful, what would my status be now? Have these trials been clear and convincing to the masses. And if so, then only I know that this society is in trouble."*

"On the other hand, what is clear and convincing? Where does one go for solace when they have the only clear and convincing personal facts, but could not convey it to believability? If that Jewell guy (the limo driver) had not had so many witnesses, he would not only have not-been-able to get his name back, he would be on death row—that would have been better for me. I'm at the other end of that spectrum, and I thought I was too smart for this. Perhaps if I had remained married to Marguerite—my first wife—this part of my life would have never happened. Perhaps stepping outside of my cocoon was a drastic mistake." Simpson may have had some dialogue with himself, like the above—perhaps not. For sure he has been thinking, murmuring and mumbling something—something that he is trying to make some sense of.

THE THIRD TRIAL

*The Third Trial already had a destiny of it's own before it began. Many were in accord with the tactics associated with this trial to satisfy the minds of many. They wanted closure for themselves. They wanted **responsibility**. Others were not, but wanted fair play within the system. They felt in this trial they were experiencing unfairness in their justice system. They had seen it before. They believed what the American Indians believed—that the white man was continuing to speak with a forked tongue. Others didn't know what to believe, they wanted fulfillment—bias or not. Fulfillment was their forte.*

Yet, others craved the excitement of a fallen Black icon. Each had a reason for the attention they had given to this notorious and infamous icon—as it was.

I thought in my heart of hearts, that I wanted to convey love, peace, strength, and justice—but my bias was not without human frailties as well. I wanted it to be fair; also, I was seeking a win for the history books however—that they would give us one out of the many who were still hanging on many tree limbs in my mind, and that they were very much unwarranted, and unfairly decreed. Yes . . . I was asking what was fair in an adversary system of justice. What I say or how I say it can be questionable and detrimental to me and it may be very different from what I really feel in my heart or even how I operate my daily activities. These are viable Q & A's, viable thoughts, and viable discussions and we are less than human beings when we deny these issues. False in one is perhaps, false in all. That is what they alluded to in the trial. If we have lied in the past, we are lying now. My God—my cups runneth over and know doubt others were pouring.

Each of us is left with our own personal evaluations, based on our biases, and that is very sad. But in all honesty, until someone admits to the crime, we will never know for sure and it seems that it is all left to God's retribution. That is why we have an adversary system of justice I suppose. They say it's fair and it produces the best justice possible. That it also produces closure—for the books and for the records—at least. In the minds and hearts of many, this case will never be closed.

Standing—I was standing—nearby others, who were in conversation. I heard one person allude to these words. "Our society and its systems have gone awry"—nuts is a better depiction. When they wanted John the Baptist's head on a platter—they got it. When they wanted Jesus crucified—they got it. When they wanted Joan of Arc burned at the stake—they got it. When they wanted Dr. John Sheppard incarcerated, in lieu of the one armed killer—they got it. When they wanted Medger Evers, or Martin Luther King Dead—well!! Time was on the side of the wicked—who had time to **burn**."

As I write this book, President Barack Obama is getting the treatment that is very similar with some issues discussed in this book—*color*.

So where are we now? The angry verdict attained in the O.J. Simpson Third Trial, had furthered polarized this nation—in more ways than one. It should be made clear that the concerns with minorities were never about Simpson necessarily. It had always been about fair play, love, equality, divinity—the things that make up a part of a democratic civilization, the things that separate us from barbarism. The Simpson case had been a circus of sorts however. It will continue to be a side show with the media. That is how they make their living and it is their right. It is the **First Amendment**.

Part II

It is not illogical for many to accept the fact that there was some truth to the now infamous Rev. Wright's statement—at least for many of us. He had said "God damn America" . . . and yes . . . we know that he left out the 'is damning America' for its way; but the meaning is very much the same. It is very hard for hardcore types in America to soften their hearts to an honest Christian side of the pulpit . . . that "something is wrong' in America with many of its extremist.

Perhaps a better comparison and seeming acceptable—and yet to mire the air waves—should be notable and stated. Do you remember the lyric change in the song at the end of the movie 'Game Change'? The Country singer said in the song "God bless America; See all the trouble she's in." This very lyric in that song was very much the same as Rev Wright was saying in his sermon. Far Right Extremist will want to see it different . . . Why . . . because this man was who he is and who he was for . . . the candidate Barack Obama.

Our ways cannot continue to negate our country nor one race of people. It just cannot continue to happen—especially when we understand the history of scripture and now America,

Americans, and what it was meant to stand for; and all that we have done to get where we are . . . well it should be said that, positive directions grows *very unlikely each and every day as polarization remains heartfelt for so many. It is hard for me to believe that God is accepting our ways as a nation and will have to damn us just as scripture has indicated end times for this earth.*

Our most basic of who we are as a nation and human rights is the question of scripture, "Did we feed the poor, do we love God with all of our hearts, and our neighbor as we love ourselves". We simply have not grown in the basics ways of Christianity and as the rich get richer and the poor get poorer, and we lose our middle class, we are sure to lose our Christian ways. Fair distribution in the financial marketplace is underwater and upside down. This will make the difference and America will lose—that is no doubt. If Middle America loses, America loses and Satan wins.

Our history is not a stellar one know matter how we might write our history books; and along the way we have gathered personalities and actions beyond belief. Reverend Wright—the minister who counseled Barack Obama with scripture before he became president—was speaking to those various actions that we have taken on overtime instead of having upgraded our behaviors and as a minister he was speaking deliberate words that even God himself would have said to Moses if had been necessary; but simply said, "Moses you will not be going over to the Promised Land. God did not like Moses temper in striking the rock for water. May

God continue to bless us, because our tempers or out of control.

Here's one . . . Black and Brown profiling, recording them into the system, jailing is a disproportion high. It is outstandingly unfair and mostly drug related—usually from smoking or selling marijuana. The problem is . . . records show that more white girls and boys use and sell this product in proportionate higher number, but are targeted in very small numbers. The statistic is most relevant to college students across the nation. Cop create a record on the black or brown person or student and in many cases will eliminate their future with a record, while white boys and girls in many, many cases are given a pass—a pass to their future.

We all know the statistics as does Reverent Wright. Little can be done in Satan's world. Others are waiting for "Thy kingdom to come, and Thy will be done on earth as it is heaven;" and this is what Rev Wright was speaking to. Perhaps I will be pillaged for saying what most will not want to hear, but Gods word has to be noted to the world. He made disciples of each of us, so will be and others will not.

Well . . . so now that we are here in America and having been protected through several wars and many trials and tribulations, we have to ask ourselves, are we getting any better with the one commandment that Jesus made so vital to our survival toward a good life and eternity . . . ? "To love our neighbors as we love ourselves?" The answer is forever an unequivocal 'not possible' answer. Americans are in love with money, tangibles, things, etc. I would say, no . . . perhaps Rev Wright would say, Satan has most of them right where he wants them. That is why some of us got what Rev Wright was saying before, but have been quashed to quietness by the power of having to survive in a world where the power of money, resources and controls remain in Satan's hands.

Blacks, or African Americans were slave in the past to a kind of greed that Satan proposed to Jesus on the mountain top—promising Jesus this world if he would just succumb to him, in many ways Native Americans had to succumb to life as they knew it in their past, in order to survive millenniums of hardships. This is not what many will want to hear, even as many others know this to be the truth.

The facts are, we don't love each other and thus we hardly love God—as Jesus says in scripture, if you do love me, you will keep my commandment—and yes! Many have died in this country keeping that commandment for others, Blacks, Native Americans, Jews, people in other lands, and what is right about that commandment. Many are stepping in line very cautiously, because they too know that Satan is tracking the good, since he has conquered the others. Oh yes, we say it, 'that we love our neighbors' but deep down we know who we really honor and what is our god.

So it was painful for so called patriots to hear a minister tell us the truth from his podium. To have the gall to acted in a positive manner to this message was something that Satan was not going to stand for, and that is why most lashed out so violently at this man and the president at that time—President Barack Obama—and is why our Jurist Prudence System has too often bent itself toward injustice; and is why Reverend Wright had every right to send a message to power in this country 'to let our people go'. Reverent Wright was speaking to the devil, and the Satin spoke back loud and clear, not to give his right of control.

Here are the facts of this matter of ownership. You cannot steal property from others unlawfully—make your laws to accommodate your wrong doings—and when others steal from you legislate a penalty of law to incarcerate that person for unending lengths of time. Laws that have been set up by man may endure to accommodate the wrong doer. The nature of Reverent Wright is to preach scripture. Scripture would say that the carpetbagger is wrong, and yes the ones stealing from the carpetbagger is also wrong. However, two wrongs do not make it right.

This is why so many were so passionate about Simpsons Trial, they just wanted for once, to see justice played out the other way around—just once in a country where even the Native American stood no chance of favoritism to his land. This profile case was to be a sign for blacks that injustice could perhaps be fair played on both sides of this wrong doing playing field. But as the cliché' would have it, "that If you give them an inch, they will take a mile." There in lye American justice.

I don't won't to deny proper recognition in how great this land has become, but I will not forget that our greatness had to have come from the facts that it was 'In God that we trusted'. I am sure that Blue Belly wealth would have everyone believe that they did it all by themselves. It is easy to think this way after one has attained high positions in life. However, I am sure that most were very humble in those hard times when they were scratching their way to the top—or perhaps not. We must not forget who this land belongs to at the present. Satan has always been there to help the crook in times of trials . . . However, Christ has been there to compromise the grateful. It has always be a sort of balance going on in this land that God has provided for us in somewhat an unlikely way. The problem is . . . many have forgotten who is in charge—others could care less because their god is seems to be winning the war. Christian knows who will win out in the end and their strength and patience will not be without rewards.

Part III

By the time the third trial had logged its verdict, Simpson had been demonized, pillaged and defamed. He was no angel. For that matter, none of us are angels in Gods eyesight. With Gods petitioning love for many disciples, may in the end prove to be fewer than assumed. Few are the Sister Theresa types either. She, like Joan of Arc, would have had little to no chance of acquittal by the end of this trial. Yes! Many were out to get him. When the first and second trial didn't accomplish the goals of those who thought they were mostly right, concerned blacks had to get back until this trial achieved its destination—white mans justice this group would soon call the third trial. Jim Crow Laws seem to have been the principles at this juncture for them. Later on, when civility has set in, history will step up to the plate to analyze some recklessness of many meticulous behaviors in this case. Some already have.

Here's was the rub on friendships, working buddies, and other latten and improved relationships in our society at the time as we were slowly moving forward; they were to remain contentious and vulnerable. If the other person expressed other than ones belief and 'status quo'—whatever that may mean—they were considered ogres. The 'status quo' type seemed distal to other than their views and was focused on only one destination—revenge. There was no other ideology for them and many blew the loudest horn.

There also had been TV's, Helicopters, Videos, Shows, Media blitz, media blitz, and more media blitz. Media was exercising the power of capitalism and 'status quo.' Multi billions of dollars passed hand to hand, aimed to show this man onerous, as if we all were not occasionally. Segments of these groups carried the longest sticks, had the deepest pockets, and had status quo on their side. They somehow felt representative of a great land, sometimes leaving out "Love of Neighbor" & "In God We Trust" edging the country even further toward polarization. Nations were watching America's duplicity.

*Yet—and somehow—saneness hovered over many in their darkness to dimness as we move toward the dawn of light. Most are awaiting our turn to express a need for luminosity and to elect a Christian light—It being a notable illumination for many Americans. Many judging only if they were being judged and recognizing that, retribution belongs to the Lord in all cases and not to Caesar. Reminiscent of our Sundays, recognizing our segregated love, and analyzing our fair play and honorable thoughts accordingly. Surely this practice would soon put each of us collectively on the winning team—the real Dream Team. Then and only then will there be vigilance, a group out there . . . waiting . . . many with candles . . . just waiting to say—not in the words of **Dr. Henry Lee**, the forensic expert—that "**Something is wrong!**" But in the words many would love to hear, that "**Something is right!**"*

AUTHOR: Clarence G. Hanley

Other Books of Clarence G. Hanley

AN ODE TO SATIRE
Clarence G. Hanley - Author
ISBN: 978-1-4259-9435-8 (sc)

SANAE MENTIS
Clarence G. Hanley - Author
ISBY: 978-1-4343-8751-6 (sc)

MY FATHER, ME
Clarence G. Hanley - Author
ISBN: 978-1-4535-1061-2
XLIBRIS CORPORATION